SWITCH

Published in Canada by Red Deer Press, 195 Allstate Parkway, Markham, Ontario L3R 4T8
Published in the United States by Red Deer Press, 311 Washington Street, Brighton, Massachusetts 02135

www.reddeerpress.com

10 9 8 7 6 5 4 3 2 1

Red Deer Press acknowledges with thanks the Canada Council for the Arts, and the Ontario Arts Council for their support of our publishing program. We acknowledge the financial support of the Government of Canada through the Canada Book Fund (CBF) for our publishing activities.

ONTARIO ARTS COUNCIL
CONSEIL DES ARTS DE L'ONTARIO
an Ontario government agency
un organisme du gouvernement de l'Ontario

Canada Council
for the Arts

Conseil des Arts
du Canada

Library and Archives Canada Cataloguing in Publication
Davey, Douglas, 1971-, author
    Switch / Douglas Davey.
Issued in print and electronic formats.
ISBN 978-0-88995-524-0 (pbk.).-- ISBN 978-1-55244-340-8 (epub).--
ISBN 978-1-55244-341-5 (pdf)
    I. Title.
PS8607.A7645S85 2014   jC813.'6   C2014-904732-0
                              C2014-904733-9

Publisher Cataloging-in-Publication Data (U.S.)
Davey, Douglas.
    Switch / Douglas Davey.
[256] pages : cm.
Summary: Sheldon Bates is a seventeen-year-old boy who realizes he is bisexual. When he comes out to his school he becomes the target of vicious abuse from his peers. Cleverly structured with footnote comments from Sheldon, now an adult, the novel shows the boy's courage at overcoming his own doubts and the prejudices of others.
ISBN-13: 978-0-88995-524-0 (pbk.)
Also published in electronic formats.
1. Bisexual high school students – Juvenile fiction. 2. Victims of abuse– Juvenile fiction. I. Title.
[Fic] dc23   PZ7.D3849Sw 2014

Edited for the Press by Kathy Stinson
Text and cover design by Daniel Choi
Cover art by Richard Gokool
Cover image courtesy of Shutterstock
Printed in Canada by Friesens Corporation

MIX
Paper from
responsible sources
FSC® C016245
www.fsc.org

SWITCH

DOUGLAS DAVEY

Red Deer Press

DEDICATION

To LGBTQ kids whenever, wherever, however.

EPIGRAPH

My candle burns at both ends;
It will not last the night;
But ah, my foes, and oh, my friends—
It gives a lovely light!

—Edna St. Vincent Millay "First Figs" from *A Few Figs from Thistles*

Part One[1]

Chapter One

This is how it began:

"Hey, guy," he asked me, "are we supposed to do full contact or just practice?"

"Full," I lied.

I said it before I had a chance to think, before I even knew what I was saying, or why I was saying it. I lay down on the tiled surface of the pool deck and looked up at my new rescue partner.

---

1 Hi, my name is Sheldon Bates. I started writing this in 1988, when I was seventeen years old, and finished it a few months later. I don't know who I wrote it for. Myself, I guess. Back then I would have rather died a million painful deaths than let anyone read it. Now that some time has gone by, and I've been given the chance to share my story, I can't pass up the opportunity. I transcribed it, (my original was handwritten), fixed up the writing a bit (some of it was almost illegible), and changed most of the names (but some are just too good to mess with). Then I added these footnotes whenever I felt the need to comment on something, which I often did, as shutting up is something I was never very good at.

Why had I said it?

He put his lips over mine, exhaling forcefully, the air from within his body filling my lungs. My chest rose and fell on its own. For a few precious seconds he breathed for me, his mouth clamped over mine. After a time, he stopped and turned his head so that his ear hovered over my mouth. He listened for a while and then rocked back on his heels.

"I guess you're going to be OK," he said, reaching out a hand to pull me into a sitting position. He was naked except for a red Speedo. He had the body of a man, his muscles clearly visible under his skin. Even though I was seventeen and had been swimming hard for years, I still looked like an elongated ten-year-old boy and my so-called physique bore all the hallmarks of a life spent avoiding work, sunlight, heavy lifting, and food. I felt awkward sitting next to him, skinny as I was, and wearing a pair of cheap and bulky swim shorts.

He told me his name and I told him mine. He was very friendly. He had strawberry blond hair, and smooth reddish skin.

"What grade are you in?" he asked.

"Twelve," I replied.

"Me too," he said.

I couldn't believe it.

How can we be the same age?

"Cool," I said, but felt far from it. "Are you in this swim class now?"

"Nah, I had to miss mine this week. They let me make it

up with this one."

A sharp voice from the far side of the pool barked out: "Front and center! Move it!" It was Rosa, my instructor. She was five curvaceous feet of olive brown skin and long black hair. She always wore sunglasses, even inside, and always took great pleasure in bossing us around.

The boy, who I thought had been a man, held out his hand for me and hoisted me up to standing. We began walking toward the side of the pool where our class gathered.

Rosa said, "I don't have all day, brats. Let's move it!"

We picked up our pace and he whispered to me, "Is she always like this?"

"Pretty much," I replied, "She's ... legendary."

Rosa must have heard us talking, because she shouted "Listen up!" and lobbed a life ring right at my head. I raised my hands to block it, and the ring struck my forearms before tumbling to the ground and rolling away. Rosa and the rest of the class laughed while I burned with embarrassment. She pulled this kind of stuff all the time, but today, standing beside this guy, I felt particularly self-conscious and more than a little ticked off.

"You two done?" she asked.

"Yeah," I answered.

After another forty-five minutes of being ordered around, we headed to the change rooms.

But wait, I'm getting ahead of myself.

In those remaining forty-five minutes of class, my mind was turned upside down. I loved girls. I loved the way they looked, the way they smiled, and the way they moved in their swimsuits. I even loved Rosa, as long as she wasn't yelling at me specifically. [2] And I loved to kiss them and to do even more with them, when I could, not that I had that much experience. But I had lied to a complete stranger, a guy, in order to have him kiss me.[3]

Sure, I said to myself, *I've noticed guys that were good looking, but I'm not gay.*

Unwanted thoughts began to push their way out from a lair at the back of my brain. They wanted me to see something, to know something, but I wouldn't let them. I shoved them all back to their hiding place so I didn't have to think about them anymore.

I'm not gay!

I don't look like it, or act like it.[4]

And I love girls! Imagine a hot girl walking away from you. What do you see? Her cute butt. Now that's sexy. OK, so now imagine some dude walking away. What do you see now? Just some dude, right?

Right?

Right?

Rosa ordered one person from each pair of rescue partners to move out of sight, then told the rest of us to lie face down in the water, trying not to breathe, pretending we'd just drowned. I got into position and waited for my new rescue partner to dive in, take me in his arms, and drag me to safety.

---

2 She was crazy-mean. Why did I find her so strangely attractive?
3 Or at least have him put his mouth onto mine. Close enough.
4 Mmm ... maybe more than I thought I did.

After class, we headed to back to the change room. I became acutely aware of him, of wanting to keep looking at him, but not too obviously. I mean, I didn't want to seem gay or anything. Unfortunately for me,[5] he was one of those guys who, even at the age of seventeen, was so comfortable with himself that he could walk around naked in front of other people and not blink an eye. He sat down next to me and struck up a conversation as we toweled off. I tried to keep my eyes way above the waistline.

"You work?" he asked.

"No, my parents want me to focus on school."

"Cool," he said. "I work for my dad's framing business."

"That's cool," I said, trying to seem nonchalant. "I bet you get to hang out with a lot of artist-types."

"Not really, just architects and engineers." He paused for a moment. "Wait, did you think it was like a picture framing business? It's house framing."

"Oh," I said, pretending I understood.

"You know, we make the wooden frames for houses?"

Oh ...

He scrubbed his short hair with the towel, then dropped it loosely around his shoulders. "It's pretty good. You get to work outside and with your hands. Most of the guys are pretty cool. If you own your own business and work hard, you can make some decent coin. Depending on when he retires, I'll either take over my dad's business or start my own somewhere else."

"My brother wants to be an architect."

---

5 Or not.

"That's the real money," he replied, and began pulling on his clothes.

When he was dressed, he said a quick goodbye and left, leaving me alone on the bench, wondering what the hell had just happened.[6]

---

6 I feel obliged to jump in here and break some news to you: if you're expecting some great romance to form between this guy and me, I'm sorry to disappoint. I only ever saw him once and I doubt he even remembers the events I'm describing. But he was kind, beautiful, and gracious enough to give me, unknowingly, my first gay kiss. I may have lost his name to the sands of time, but I'll never forget him.

Chapter Two

I called out, "Yo, Jenny!" She turned to see me and smiled. She was halfway down the hall, getting her stuff together for first period.

"Hi, Shelly!" she replied.[7]

"How's it going?" I asked.

"Awesome."

It was great to see her again. After what had happened in the pool, I'd been really second-guessing myself but, as soon as I saw her, I knew it must have been a fluke.

She's so cute!

And what a totally hot body!

Jen waved a hand in front of my face. "Hello? Stare much?"

"What?" I replied, slightly dazed.

---

7 Shelly was her nickname for me. I didn't like it, but she made out with me at least once a week so I wasn't going to do anything to jeopardize that.

"You just went out-of-body on me."

"Oh, sorry. I was deep in thought."

"Yeah, right."

"Wow, what a nice girlfriend I have. Not."[8]

"Kidding!" she said and flashed me a cute smile. Sure, it was kind of fake, but I was helpless to resist. "Did you go to swimming last night?"

"Uh ... yeah."

"Was the sexy one there?" she asked coyly.

Sexy one?

For a panicked second I thought that Jen had somehow found out about the guy at the pool. Then I realized that she meant Rosa. I'd made the mistake of telling Jen about how hot I thought my coach was, and now she always teased me about liking her.

"Yeah, I guess."

"You're not sure?"

"Sure of what?"

"That she was there, idiot!"

"Yeah, absolutely. It was just, like, a ... a long time ago."

Keep it together, man!

"Omigod, Shelly. It was just last night. What the hell's wrong with you today?"

"Nothing. I'm just tired."

"I hope you're not sick or anything. You probably got something from the pool. That place is gross."

It was kind of gross, but I didn't feel like agreeing with her. "I'm fine. The pool's fine. It's so chlorinated, nothing

---

8 Sticking "Not" at the end of a sarcastic line was something we picked up from *Saturday Night Live* and was a well-established joke.

could possibly live in it."

"All those chemicals are bad for your hair." She reached up and patted the short, unhealthy mess on top of my head.

I reached up and took hold of her hand. "It's fine, I promise." I pulled her in close and gave her a kiss on the cheek.

"Meet at lunch?" she asked.

"Yeah, sure."

She started to walk away, but turned, squinting her eyes and pointing a warning finger at me. It was one of her signature moves. "Don't forget!"

"I won't."

"'Cause I need help with trig."

"No problem."[9]

As she turned and walked away, I stared at her butt, which was attractively fitted into pale blue jeans and moved hypnotically from side-to-side as she walked. Just looking at it was killing me.

Man, oh, man, I thought. *I am definitely not gay.*

I headed to class, but stopped when I saw something going on ahead of me, some kind of scuffle. Two guys, maybe Grade 10's, had grabbed some Grade 9 kid who looked like he was about eight years old and had him pushed up against a locker. The few people left in the thinning crowd either didn't notice or didn't care. I wasn't the coolest kid in the school,[10] and definitely not the toughest,[11] but I *was* one of the tallest, and felt like I didn't have to take crap off

9 School, especially math, came so easily to me that I never really had to develop good study habits. This turned disastrous in university.
10 Understatement.
11 Mega understatement.

of anyone.[12] I walked right up and slammed my hand on the locker beside one of the older kids. He jumped, just like I knew he would.

"What the hell, man?" I demanded. They all looked at me, probably thinking I was a teacher or something.[13] I could tell from their expressions that the bullies wanted to tell me off, maybe even try to take shot at me, but they thought better of it.

"But he's ..."

I cut him off. "I don't give a damn! Get lost before I drag your ass down to the office!"

I heard one of them mutter something as they dropped the kid and stormed off. Without a word, the kid they were picking on gathered his stuff from the floor, then ran down the hallway, disappearing out of sight.

You're welcome, kid.

Like every day at lunch, Jen and I met in the cafeteria, eating alongside Sarah and Dan. Because they lived so close to each other, Dan would often give Sarah a ride when she needed it, but, as they liked to remind everyone, they "weren't going out." It made sense, actually; they were almost exact opposites. Sarah was loud and obnoxious; Dan was quiet and cool. They were both funny but in totally different ways.

I told everyone the story of the kid and the bullies. When I was done, I said, "... and that's how I totally saved this kid's life."

---

12 Oh, I was so wrong.
13 Highly unlikely!

"What'd you do that for?" Jenny said, dunking a French fry into a pool of ketchup on her paper plate.

"Uh, geez, Jenny, I don't know. Maybe it was because a couple of jerks were going to beat up a little kid."

"Well, you didn't really help him."

"What are you talking about? I stopped him from getting his ass kicked!"

"You *know* they're just gonna get him worse later. And now he doesn't know how to stick up for himself."

"Easy for you to say. You never had a bunch of guys twice your size gang up on you."

Sarah snorted and said, "She wishes."

"Sarah?" Jen said, a super-big, super-fake smile plastered across her face. "Go to hell."

Sarah tilted her head to one side and returned the smile.

Jen looked at me and her voice became unusually serious. "I had to stand up for myself plenty of times. Grade 9's really hard. The guys are immature jerks and the girls are the biggest bitches on the planet."

"I remember," Sarah added.

"See?" Jen said, gesturing toward her friend.

But Sarah added, "How can I forget? You were the biggest bitch of all."

"Very funny," Jenny said.

"You were *such* a bitch that you called me a 'slut' for holding a boy's hand. Meanwhile, you let that guy from the French school feel you up, even though you didn't have anything to feel."

Jenny threw a fry at Sarah. "Shut up!"

Sarah flinched as it hit her shirt. "Gross!" She flicked it away with the back of her hand.

They were always arguing like that. I thought it was funny, even though every once in a while one of them would take it too far and the other would get angry.

"It's not the same," I said, bringing the conversation back on track. "Being teased is one thing, but being beat up is another. I remember some guys helped me out when I was younger."

Dan poked a finger into my bony chest. "And look at you now. You're a useless idiot."

"Nice. What a supportive friend you are. Not."

Jen said, "I'm just saying, you can't be there every day to help that kid out."

"And I'm saying, I can't believe I helped this kid out and no one thinks it was the right thing to do. Dan, back me up here."

Dan leaned back and said, "I was too cool to get beaten up, even when I was a minor niner."

"Yeah," I said, "Doing your shirt buttons all the way up to the collar. Real cool. Chicks dig that."

Sarah snorted with laughter. "You totally used to do that. What a nerd!"

We all laughed and the topic changed, but I kept thinking about that kid.

I did the right thing, helping him out, didn't I?

Chapter Three

After lunch I had a spare period,[14] which meant I didn't have to rush out to class. After we said our goodbyes, everyone filed out of the caf, and I was left alone in the big empty room. When my friends were with me, Jenny especially, I wasn't so worried about what had happened at swimming. I could just not think about it. But when I was alone, with no one else to distract me, thoughts of the guy from the pool were creeping back in. I knew that I was definitely still hot for Jenny, but I couldn't get this other guy out of my head. Whenever I thought of him, thoughts would buzz around in the back of my mind.

The whole thing was scaring me to death.

But I had a plan, and the very fact of having one made me feel a little bit better. It gave me something to do, and it was

---

14 Thanks to taking a super-easy extra credit course the summer before.

a relief to actually be taking steps to solve my problem.

Here was the situation: I loved girls (in general) and Jenny (in particular). Girls were often cute, sometimes sexy, and almost always smelled good. When I saw a hot one, I got this feeling. It was hard to describe. But then there was this one guy who gave me that same kind of feeling.

One of those buzzing thoughts flitted forward.

Are you sure there's really only one guy?

I brushed the thought away like a pesky insect. I couldn't't deal with it. I had a dilemma to solve: Am I gay or not?

Thinking back to a time when I was actually paying attention in class,[15] I remembered a teacher asking something like, "What do you do when faced with an unknown?" The answer was to conduct an experiment: hypothesis, test, and conclusion.

The hypothesis: There is a slight chance, a very slight chance, a tiny, remote, highly unlikely chance that I might, *might*, be gay.

The test: Well, there's a bunch of ways to test that, but I picked one that didn't involve touching anyone. The plan, such as it was, was to stare at guys and see if I thought any of them were sexually attractive. Not just good looking in a general sense, like a movie star,[16] but actually someone I could see myself kissing.

Then, I would reach the conclusion: I'm gay or I'm not.[17]

---

15 Rare.

16 Many straight guys have an amusingly hard time admitting which movie stars, etc., they find attractive, as they fear it will make them look gay.

17 Ok, time out. I feel like I have to stop here and explain how I could be so obviously bisexual and still refuse to recognize it or even consider it as a possibility. The first thing is, as far as I knew, being gay meant spending your life being hated, ridiculed, ostracized, and living under the constant threat of violence. So it's no

I came up with an experiment that was as scientific as possible. It was totally objective.[18] I even worked out a methodology, just like in class. First, I came up with a secret code for recording my data, just in case anyone saw my notebook and figured out what I was doing.[19] I decided to write a "D" (for "dude") when I saw a guy and a "C" (for "chick") when I saw a girl. Sure, I could have used M for male and F for female, but I thought that was too obvious.

Once I'd noted what sex they were, I'd determine whether or not I thought they were hot. I'd write a plus sign (+) if I liked them, and a minus sign (-) if I didn't. When I was done, all I'd have to do was compare the plusses[20] and the minuses. If there were more plusses under the girls than the boys, then there was no problem. I was straight.[21] Case closed. The guy at the pool was just a fluke. If there were more plusses under the guys' side, I was in trouble.

There was just one little problem with my experiment: I didn't want to do it. If I took my test, I'd find out which side of the fence I fell on, and I felt like I'd rather be dead than fall on the "wrong" side.

But there was no putting it off; I had to do it.

---

surprise that I was dedicated to *not* being gay. I was so dedicated, in fact, that I deluded myself into accepting some pretty flawed logic: if people are either straight or gay (false) and I like girls (true, but with an error of omission—I liked guys, too), then I am straight (false). I didn't realize that I was creating what logicians call an "either-or fallacy." There were more than two possibilities (straight or gay); I just refused to see them. I wasn't aware of bisexuality as a viable consideration. I knew the word and the concept, but the only bi person I'd ever heard of was David Bowie and he was a rock star. I'm going to stop now because this footnote has gotten out of hand.

18 Hardly.

19 Something I cribbed from da Vinci.

20 This is how you spell the plural of "plus." Doesn't it look weird?

21 The either-or fallacy strikes again.

I had to know the truth. I sat myself down in the main foyer. I took my notebook in my hand and said a little desperate prayer to any god that would listen.

Please please please let me not be gay ...

The first person to pass was a guy, younger than me. He was wearing jeans, black running shoes, and a T-shirt. His hair was messy and pushed up in the front like he'd licked his hand and run it up his forehead. Looking at him I felt ... nothing.

No attraction, I observed, trying to retain the cool objectivity of a scientist examining a petri dish. With a substantial amount of relief, I marked my notebook with a D-.

A girl walked by.

Yes! I thought. *Here's my chance to really prove this thing.*

Like the guy before her, she was younger than me. She was kind of short, and her bangs had been hair-sprayed upwards into a gravity-defying reverse waterfall.[22] I wanted to like her, I really did, but I had to be honest with myself or else the test would fall apart.

Rating: C-.

Might as well be an f.

F for Fail.

F for Fairy.

F for Fruit.

F for Faggot.

It wasn't going like I'd hoped. For one thing, there simply weren't enough people in the hallway. I needed a bigger

---

22 A style that was popular with fans of so-called "hair metal."

sample. I had just started to record that fact in my notebook when I was startled by a female voice.

"What are you sitting on the floor for?"

I looked up and saw Stephanie. She was in my grade but we'd never talked much.

"Oh, hi, Steph."

"What's going on?" she asked.

It occurred to me that I should have come up with a cover story to explain what I was doing.

"Oh, I just thought I'd, y'know, work out here. It's ... quieter."

"Isn't the floor cold? You get hemorrhoids from sitting on cold floors, y'know."[23]

"No, I'm fine."

"Whatever. See ya." She walked away. I'd never really felt any attraction to her, but I had to admit that she had nice legs *and* she had VPL.[24]

Rating: C+.

yes!!!

I spent the rest of the hour evaluating anyone and everyone who walked by: students, teachers, cleaning staff, you name it. I rated them all. When I had rated forty people, I examined the results: fifteen C+'s, eight C-'s, and seventeen D-'s.

I did some quick math.

---

23 You can't get hemorrhoids from sitting on cold floors. And that's how you spell "hemorrhoids," which I think is even weirder than "plusses."

24 AKA Visible Panty Lines, i.e., you could see the outline of her underwear through her jeans. Many girls hate the word "panties" for some reason, so please do not irritate them by saying it over and over and over ...

D+	0	0.0%
D-	17	42.5%
C+	15	37.5%
C-	8	20.0%
TOTAL	40	100.0%

See, I told myself, *numbers don't lie: 0% attraction to males, 37.5% attraction to females. What happened in the pool was a one-off, just a weird thing. The kind of thing that they say in health class is nothing to worry about. Besides, people don't suddenly become gay, do they? It's not like turning on a light switch. And besides, I've never had a gay thought in my life before the pool.*[25]

Out of the corner of my eye, I saw the wide, fringed oval of a janitor's broom.

A deep voice said, "Don't worry, I can sweep around you."

I looked up and saw a janitor I didn't recognize, which was weird because I thought I knew everyone who worked at the school. He was tall and tanned, maybe forty-five years old, with long, thinning hair pulled into a short ponytail. His sleeves were rolled up. When he gripped the broom handle, the muscles of his forearms stood out like cables under his skin. He had knuckle tattoos that said "ROCK" and "ROLL."

All the custodians had to wear a uniform, but somehow he made his look cool. Maybe it was because of the way his shirt pulled tightly across his broad shoulders. Or how he wore it half-unbuttoned over a classic white undershirt.

25 Reader, there is a slight chance, a very slight chance, a tiny, remote, highly unlikely chance that I might, *might*, have been lying to myself. Actually, it's more like a 100% chance.

Whatever it was, he was pretty much the coolest guy I had ever seen.

"Getting some work done?" he asked.

"Yeah," I croaked.

"I know why you like to sit on the hall floor," he said with a devilish grin.

I began to panic again, afraid that I was found out.

"Checkin' the girlies out, I bet! You get a good view up any skirts down there?"

Oh ... phew.

"Heh. Yeah," I said, trying to sound casual.

"I was a teenager once, too." He leaned over. In a conspiratorial tone, he added, "Hell, I'm still checkin' the girlies out. And there is some mighty fine skirt[26] 'round here, let me tell you."

I didn't know how else to reply. I was never any good at this kind of guy talk. I just said, "Yeah."

"'Course, with my job and my age, it's 'look but don't touch,' am I right?"

"Uh ... right."

"So, you got a girl?"

I couldn't answer, my thoughts were a jumble.

Why are you talking to me? What should I say? Why can I not stop staring at that deep indentation where his neck meets his chest?[27]

"Yeah," I said after a pause.

"You sure about that?"

"Yeah. Her name's Jenny. She's ..."

---

26 I came to learn that he had a big repertoire of vintage slang.
27 That's the suprasternal notch, also known as the "well." Thanks, Wikipedia.

She's what?

"... she's got long brown hair." It was the best I could do.

"She do the wild thing?"

I almost choked.

He laughed, "Hell, I'm just messing with ya, brother." He lowered his voice to a near-whisper. "You get high?"

"Sure."

Once. Then I tried to ride home and fell off my bike.

"Right on. I just started here. You need anything, you come see me, all right? But keep it on the QT.[28] Cool?"

"Sure ... cool."

"I'll see ya 'round, brother." He walked away, pushing his broom and whistling.

He was more than twice my age, a rockabilly[29] dude with a balding ponytail. But he had these funny blue eyes, a strong nose, and there was something about the proportion of his body—shoulders, waist, legs—that was incredibly magnetic. I imagined him embracing me with those big arms and I knew it was something that I could handle.

Something I would welcome.

Reluctantly, I put a single D+ in my notebook.

D for Dude.

D for Damn.

Damn. Damn. Damn.

---

28 Meaning, keep it to yourself.
29 Part rocker, part hillbilly. Early Elvis Presley is the best example I can think of.

Chapter Four
_____

Over the phone, Jen's voice was growing agitated. "Yeah, but why? I don't even get how trig works."

I was supposed to be helping with her math homework, but between my frayed nerves (which I couldn't possibly explain) and her TV, which was blaring away in the background, I was in no mood to help anyone with anything.

"I don't know," I lied. "Just ... memorize SOH–CAH–TOA."[30]

"But how am I supposed to memorize it if I don't even know what it means?"

"I don't know!" I said. "Just memorize it."

"That's real helpful. Thanks a lot."

There was a burst of canned laughter from her TV.

_____
30 Classic memorization tool for trigonometry.

With obvious irritation, I asked her, "What are you watching?"

"*Full House*,"[31] she answered.

"That show is so stupid," I said.[32] "I think it's cute," she said sharply and hung up.

Now I'll have that to deal with tomorrow ...

As soon as she was off the phone, my mind raced back to where it had been all night: the rock-and-roll janitor and that one D+ in my notebook.

It was only one, I thought, *but isn't one all it takes to make me gay? And let's say that I really did have the hots for him, just the tiniest bit. What does that even mean? How come I'm not crushing on any guys my age? I was in love (or lust) with lots of teenaged girls, so how come no teenaged guys? Well, there was that guy at the pool, but I thought he was older than me. Can I be gay and straight?*[33]

By the start of school the next day, my brain hadn't improved. The fact that it was Friday probably didn't help. I found Jenny sitting by her locker. She looked pissed when she saw me. I took a chance and sat down beside her.

"Sorry about last night," I said.

She glared at me. "What's wrong with you?"

"I don't know. I can help you now if you want."

"Now it's too late. I have to take my stupid test first period."

"Well, I can help you after if you want."

"Great," she said, then got up and walked away.

---

31 Unbelievably saccharine yet extremely popular sit-com.
32 I'm sympathetic to my anxious mental state at the time, but I also want to go back in time and slap myself for being an ass.
33 Finally, it starts to dawn on me.

I decided to skip the cafeteria at lunch; I wasn't hungry anyway.[34] I knew that hanging out with Dan would improve my mental state, but I felt like being alone. Besides, I'd see him later in Mrs. Piedmont's English class. What I needed, even more than cheering up, was time to myself, time to think, time to figure things out. But where? In school, there's no place to go to be by yourself.

I was completely preoccupied by the inconclusive results of my not-so-scientific experiment.

I kept asking myself: *Why hadn't it worked?*[35]

I figured that I must have missed something, some tiny scrap of information that would illuminate everything. But what was it? I'd have to do more research to find out, except I wasn't sure where to go, or who to talk to when I got there. There was no way I was going approach any of the adults I knew for help. I needed something discreet, something secret, something that would give me all the information I was looking for.

I needed a book.[36]

I liked to read, mostly Stephen King, but I'd never had to do much in the way of research. I was going to have to talk to one of the school librarians. But I couldn't just waltz up to the desk and ask point blank about being gay. I had to be subtle. And, even if by some miracle I did find the perfect book, I couldn't actually borrow it. That would be suicide.

---

34 I used to throw up if I ate when I got stressed out.

35 Actually, it did work. I just wasn't ready to admit it.

36 Back in the day, information wasn't something you just acquired whenever you wanted it; it was something that had to be unearthed, usually in book form, and often with the assistance of a librarian. In some ways, the idea seems ridiculously arcane, but I kind of like it at the same time.

I pushed my fears and questions aside and approached the librarian on duty. I didn't know her name, but I'd talked to her a few times and she was always friendly. She was sitting at the help desk, staring down at a magazine, the eraser end of a pencil resting lightly between her teeth.

"Hi," I said.

She looked up at me and set the pencil down on the desk. "What can I do for you?"

"Yeah, um ... where can I go to get some ... information, I guess."

"Well, you're in the right place. What kind of information?"

I struggled to find the right words. "I don't know, just ... information."

Her expression became quizzical. I guess most people were a little more specific with their requests. She asked, "How about this: Which class is it for?"

I contemplated making something up, but knew it would only dig me in deeper. "It's just for myself."

"Do you have a specific piece of information that you're looking for?

Yes. Do you have a foolproof "Am I gay" test?

"No. Just, like, general information."

"OK ... Maybe you should start in the reference section. You know where that is?"

I probably should have but didn't. "No."

"It's just over there." She pointed to a corner of the room.

"By the encyclopedias and dictionaries and stuff?"

I knew where those were, at least.

She smiled wryly. "Those *are* the reference section."

"Oh. OK."

She made a tick mark on a piece of paper in front of her. "Come back if you need more help, OK?"

"Sure."

I went over to the reference shelf and saw that it held a couple of dictionaries, a thesaurus, and an encyclopedia set.

May as well start with the basics.

I grabbed the biggest dictionary I could find. It was a big brown monster of a book that weighed as much as your average toddler. I arranged myself so that no one could see what I was looking at, then began flipping through the G section until I found the entry for "gay."

gay (gā) adj. **1.** Happy and carefree; merry. **2.** Brightly colorful or ornamental. **3.** Jaunty; sporty. **4.** Full of or given to lighthearted pleasure. **5.** Rakish; libertine. **6.** Slang Homosexual. [< OF < Gmc.] — gay'ness n.
— **Syn. 1.** cheerful, vivacious, merry, sprightly, lively.[37]

I decided that the dictionary definitions were useless. No one used "gay" to mean "happy" anymore; "ornamental" was way off topic; and every school kid already knew that "gay" meant "homosexual."[38]

I moved on to the thesaurus. It wasn't alphabetical like the dictionary, but was organized by theme. You had to look everything up in the index. I tried "gay" again. There were

---

37 I don't remember doing it, but I must have returned to the library to transcribe this entry. There's no way I wrote all that from memory.
38 But who doesn't want to be described as "rakish"?

a lot of different sub-headings below it, each leading to its own section:

gay[39]
cheerful
colorful
convivial
festive
happy
homosexual
intoxicated
showy
unchaste

"Intoxicated" was appealing; "festive" sounded fun; but the real choice was evident. I looked up "homosexual" in the index. I found it, number 32 out of 33 listings under the category of "SEX":

Homosexual,[40] homoerotic, gay [informal], queer [derog]; **bisexual**, bisexed, epicene, AC-DC [informal], lesbian, Sapphic, tribadistic; mannish, butch, effeminate; transvestite; **perverted**

My eyes skated over the entries, stopping at that final terrible word: *perverted*. It confirmed everything I'd feared, everything I'd felt. And it was written in bold, just so I wouldn't miss the point.

That's me. That's what I am. A pervert.

---

39 Also transcribed into my notebook.
40 The words in bold are headings, meaning you can look them up for more synonyms.

In my mind, I could picture a sickening chain of words.

Perverted ... sick ... unwanted ... friendless ... hopeless ... and then ... what?

Dead?[41]

I looked back to the list. *Queer* was on there, too. I'd used that word before, along with *faggot* and *fruit*, stuff like that. But I was joking; they were just words you threw around. Now people were going to use them on me.

I'm going to be the pervert.

The queer.

The faggot.

The fruit.

The thought was nauseating. I was glad I hadn't eaten lunch.

The thesaurus gave me as many questions as answers.

What the hell does Sapphic[42] mean?

Or epicene?[43]

Are the guys from the band ac/dc gay?[44]

And why are all these words under the same heading?[45]

Is gay the same as bisexual?[46]

I had to stop and think about that. I knew they were

---

41 I should add that this was right when AIDS was hitting the mainstream news. It was a pretty scary time.

42 In this case, it means relating to lesbianism. The word comes from the Greek poet Sappho; more about her later.

43 Having both male and female qualities, or neither.

44 I don't think so. As an aside, they were the first Australian rock band I knew of. Many more were to come.

45 Good question.

46 Some people use "gay" to mean anyone with any amount of attraction to any-one of the same sex, while others use it for people who are ONLY attracted to those of the same sex. In casual conversation, I tend to mix up the use, or add qualifiers, like "100% gay."

different, but were they *really* different? Both words meant that you liked people of the same sex.

My gaze slid back to that other word in bold: **bisexual**.

What was it about that word? Maybe it was the strange assortment of letters, with that funny little x right in the middle.

X marks the spot.

I tapped it with my finger, like it was a treasure map.

Tap tap tap tap tap …

I knew I was on to something.

I switched from the thesaurus back to the big dictionary, flipping eagerly through the pages until I found what I was looking for.

bi·sex·u·al

I shivered and read the entry with eager eyes:

bi·sex·u·al (bī.sek'.shōō.əl), adj. 1. of both sexes. 2. Having the organs of both sexes; hermaphrodite. 3. Erotically attracted by both sexes. — n. **1.** A hermaphrodite. **2.** A bisexual person. — **bi.sex'u.al.ism**, **bi.sex.u.al.i.ty** (bī.sek'.shōō.al'ə.tē) n. —**bi.sex'u.al.ly** adv.

I don't know how many times I reread that third definition.

Erotically attracted by both sexes …

Somewhere in my head, gears began to connect and turn. I knew I'd found a piece of the puzzle.

Someone spoke, once again startling me.

"What are you reading the dictionary for?"

I looked up and saw this guy from my grade, Davidson.[47] I was motionless with fear, quietly panicking, terrified that I'd been found out. He stared at me, waiting for an answer. It felt like hours passed as I tried to get my brain and mouth to work in unison.

"I was just looking something up," I said.

Bored, barely interested, he asked, "What?"

"Uh ..." I looked down at the dictionary, struggling to find a word that was near *that* word but wasn't *that* word.

Bisectrix? Too close ...

Birth canal? No way ...

Birthday suit? Uh-uh ...

pick fast.

Bismuth?

Bismuth.

"Bismuth," I replied.

"What the hell's bismuth?"

I looked down and read the definition right from the page. "A lustrous, reddish white metallic element occuring native as well as in combination, used in medicine, in the manufacture of cosmetics, etc."

He looked at me like I was crazy. "What the hell d'you need to know that for?"

Why indeed?

"Because ... knowledge is power?"

What?

"What?" he asked, looking slightly confused.

---

47 We called him by his last name for some reason. This is the only time he shows up in the story. When I was piecing this together, I considered swapping him out for someone more important to the tale, but I'm trying to keep it real here, people.

Change the subject …

I asked him, "Are we playing basketball tomorrow or what?"[48]

"How the hell should I know?"

To further distract him, I decided to go on the offensive with a sarcastic attack. "What are *you* doing in the library?" I asked, as if it were the last place he'd ever visit. "*Reading?*"

"Yeah, right. I got lunch detention."

"That sucks," I replied.

"Yeah."

I closed the dictionary and placed it back on the shelf. "I gotta head out."

"See ya," he said and walked away.

I let out a long sigh.

Close one.

I headed for the door but stopped just short of leaving. It was almost like I was afraid to step into the hallway.

I wasn't too far from the librarian who had helped me earlier. She asked, "Did you find what you're looking for?"

"Yeah," I replied. "I think so."

---

48 My favorite sport to play, not because of any particular talent, but because I was already six feet tall.

Chapter Five

I headed to English, which was taught by Mrs. Piedmont.[49] I'd always found her really, really annoying.[50] She wasn't a bad teacher, not compared to some of the others I'd had, but her classes were mostly lectures, and usually boring. Her wardrobe was decades old, making her look like a relic. Worst of all, she was one of those people who seem perpetually chipper, even when they're telling you off.

She handed back our essays and gave us the usual: "You're not working up to your potential" speech. I got an A on mine. English wasn't my best subject but I still did well in it. Dan, who was sitting beside me, held up his paper. B. He shrugged his shoulders. Nothing ever got to him.

I found it hard to concentrate at the best of times, but that day was even worse. My head was spinning, thinking about

---

49 AKA "Mrs. Pee Pot." Hilarious, right?
50 Although my opinion of her would soon change.

all that had happened and all that I'd learned. The whole class was a blur. Blah blah blah ... essays ... blah blah blah ... *Hamlet* ... blah blah blah ... *Tess of the d'Urbervilles* ... blah blah blah ... speeches ...

Afterwards, Dan and I walked back to our lockers. He took the school bus, which meant he always had to hurry, but I was able to walk home and could take my time.

"You in tonight?" he asked.

Friday was our usual movie night. It seemed weird to do something so normal when my life felt so upside down, but maybe it was just what I needed.[51] And, despite everything that had happened in the last week, this Friday night was supposed to be a big one for me and Jen.[52]

"Absolutely. If I can get Jen to come. She's pissed at me."

"Why?"

"Nothing."

"Don't worry, she'll go. Sarah's going. I'm picking her up."

I'd learned not to ask why Dan and Sarah always did stuff like that when they weren't even going out. Could a guy and a girl like that really just be friends?

"I don't know. Jen's already ticked off. And if it's an action movie, she will NOT want to go."

"She'll come."

"Maybe."

"Hey," Dan said, "if the Flintstones are cavemen, how come they have dinosaurs all over the place?"[53]

---

51 Plus, despite everything, I still had big plans for afterward, as you'll soon see.
52 You'll find out why in just a little while.
53 Picking apart cartoons was a longstanding conversation topic of ours.

"Hey, yeah. I expect my cartoons to be historically accurate."

"Absolutely."

We laughed and said goodbye.

It was spring. While the air was still a little cool, especially at night, the grass was up and the sun was bright. I walked home through the park, passing the old basketball court next to the stand of trees known as the Woods. I don't know if you could actually call the Woods a forest or anything, as there were only enough trees to cover up the sight of students drinking or making out, but it was the only "woods" around. The ground inside was always muddy and littered with beer bottles and cigarette butts. When we were little, our parents told us to stay out of it, but we never did.

I made it to the sidewalk and trudged toward my suburban home.

A few houses down from my own, I passed Duncan, a schoolmate and archetypal Tech Kid.[54] He was quiet and sullen. We'd never had much to say to each other. He was kneeling beside his family's lawnmower, which was upside down, and he was doing some kind of work to the underside.

"Hey," I said as I passed. He looked up, his squinting eyes partially hidden by a curtain of shaggy black hair and the brim of a dirty baseball hat.

---

54 "Tech Kids," AKA "Techies," AKA "Techers," were students who took mostly shop classes, as opposed to those students in the academic stream, who were some-times lumped together under the names "Preps," "Preppies," or "Preppers." The two groups didn't always mix, but they weren't at war like in *The Outsiders*.

"Hey," he replied and went back to work on the lawnmower.

Duncan, you moron, you have such a simple life.[55]

I left home early in my parents' car, picked Jen up from her house out in the country, and we hit the mall so we could get some snacks for the movie.[56] The shopping center was old and rundown, but it was right beside the theater, so we usually stopped there.

Inside, we met Sarah and Dan, and I begged them to go with me to my favorite place in the mall, this terrible old department store.[57] It was full of decrepit mannequins, wildly out-of-date fashions, and brand names you'd never find anywhere else. The rear of the store, which was eerily lit by sad aquariums, was like a whole other world. I thought the place was cool in a weird kind of way, but no one else did.

As we entered the store, we passed a young woman who worked at the checkout counter. Like all the employees, she wore a blue vest. A serious-looking guy in a red beret[58] was leaning on the counter across from her, flipping through the LP's.[59]

I heard him say, "Your music selection is terrible." With obvious frustration, she said, "God! Do you have to say that every single

---

55 Not only was I was totally judgmental, I was also spectacularly wrong.
56 If movie theatres didn't charge prices that defied all theory of supply and demand, we wouldn't have to resort to sneaking our snacks in.
57 There used to be tons of these before the big box stores took over.
58 Don't be fooled; berets were definitely NOT in fashion.
59 AKALong Playing vinyl records, from back in the day when music came in containers.

time? I know how bad this place sucks."

Jenny laughed and whispered, "Even the people who work here hate this store."

Walking through the aisles with my friends, marveling at the odd and mysterious products, I felt better than I had in ages. No matter what, we were all together and life was going to carry on. I could tell Jen about what I was going through[60] and she'd take it all in stride.

We passed a doe-eyed female mannequin that looked like it was decomposing. "She" was naked and the surface of her skin was marred by chips and scrapes.

Sarah said, "That's what Barbie would look like if she was a zombie." We all laughed and then wandered into the food aisle.

My eyes fell on a colossal jar of what looked like hundreds of tiny eyeballs suspended in brackish water.

I hoisted it up for all to see. "Check it out!"

"What is that?" Jenny asked, looking disgusted.

"Three gallons of pickled onions." I replied, and held the jar out in her direction. "This store's awesome."

Jen stuck out her tongue. "Gross. Who needs three gallons of pickled onions?"

"Who needs *any* pickled onions?" Sarah replied.

I was going to reply, "People who drink a lot of cocktails?" but Dan took the jar from me and put it back on the shelf. "Can we get out of here now?"

"In a minute," I said, and headed to the back of the store.

The place had, to our knowledge, the only working

---

60 I felt very compelled to tell her, both because I needed to talk to someone, and because *not* telling her seemed dishonest. I had kissed someone else, after all.

instant photo booth in town. From a distance, and in the spooky light of the fish tanks, you might be convinced that the photo booth was new, with a kind of retro chic. But once you got closer, you'd realize that it wasn't retro, it was actually just really, really old.

I pleaded with Jenny to come in with me. "C'mon, it'll be fun!"

"No, my hair looks stupid."

"It looks fine. C'mon!" I grabbed her by the wrist and pulled her toward the heavy vinyl curtain of the photo booth.

"Ugh. Fine. But then we're leaving. I hate it in here; it's depressing."

"Deal," I said and pulled aside the curtain to let her in.

She stood hunched over in the corner while I sat down on the cracked red vinyl of the swivel stool. It was a little high so I lifted up my butt and gave the seat a twirl. Once it was low enough, I sat back down and pulled Jen across my lap.

I had to twist my hips a bit in order to dig my money out of my pocket. The movement forced Jen against the wall and she grunted in displeasure.

"Why didn't you get your quarters out before you sat down?" she asked.

The glass panel at the front of the booth doubled as a mirror. Jen leaned toward it, flicking her hair over her ears. She licked the tips of two fingers and then ran them over her eyebrows, working some secret female magic to make them look perfect. I looked into my palm to see what I'd managed to pull out of my pocket: three quarters, a few pennies, and lint.

"Jenny ..." I said sweetly.

"Ye-es," she replied, breaking the word into two syllables.

"Do you have a quarter I could borrow?"

"God!" she said in slightly amused frustration.[61] "This is the very last time I'm coming here with you. The VERY LAST TIME." She reached into her purse and dropped a quarter in my palm.

"Thanks, Jenny."

She was peeved but I didn't care. It felt so great to be there with her, doing the kinds of things we'd always done. It was like nothing had changed.

I slid the quarters into the slot one after another. When the last one fell home, the entire booth began to shimmy and shake like it was strapped to the belly of an airplane.

Jen held out a hand to steady herself. "One day this thing is going to kill someone. It better not be me."

A moment later, the shivering faded and was replaced by a low-pitched thrumming from somewhere deep in the booth. A flashing light indicated that our first shot was about to begin. We tried to change positions at the last minute, but the camera went off before we were ready.

FLASH.

"Crap," I said.

"Can we have at least one nice picture?" Jen said. We leaned in toward each other and smiled at the darkened pane of glass that hid the camera.

---

61 It was pretty much her default tone of voice.

FLASH.

"Now a serious one," I suggested, and we did our best to look solemn.

FLASH.

"Now romantic," I said and leaned in to kiss her cheek.

FLASH.

"Now I'm leaving," she said and began to get up.

I put my arm around her waist and pulled her back down to my lap. "Y'know, we are all alone in here ..."

"Please!" she said, rolling her eyes at our admittedly unromantic environment.

"Fine."

We exited the booth and waited outside the machine as it whirred and sputtered. Beside us, Sarah and Dan had stopped at a display of View-Masters.[62]

"Oh, wow!" Sarah said excitedly. "Did you ever have one of these?"

Dan nodded.

Sarah took a peek in the viewer, then brought it back down again. "It's too dark back here. We had my stepdad's. He gave them to us before he died.[63] They were soooo old. We had this one with Charlie Brown and Snoopy."

Jen said, "Ah, I love the Charlie Brown Christmas special."

"But didn't you always wonder," I asked, "if Lucy hated Charlie Brown so much, why did she put him in charge of their play?"

Dan added, "And how did the Christmas tree go from being a stick to being all, like, full and green and perfect?"

---

62 They were like little binoculars that you could look in and see pictures.
63 Her dad took off, then her mom remarried, and then that guy died. Pretty tragic.

Jen just shook her head.

Sarah said, "Maybe because Christmas is magic and it's just a stupid TV show. Anyway, the one we had wasn't a cartoon, it was all photos of puppets or something like that. We loved them." Her voice became uncharacteristically soft. "I wonder where they are? I bet my mom sold them. God, I hate her."

She stared thoughtfully at the View-Master in her hands, like it held an important secret just for her.

Behind us, a dramatic rise in pitch from the ancient photo booth let us know that it was about to give birth to our damp line of images. The machine made one final shake and then the pictures emerged. I reached into the tiny slot and picked up the strip by its edge. I thought they all looked good, except for the first one, which was mostly a dark blur made by Jen's jean jacket. I held them up for her to examine.

She looked at them distastefully, critiquing each one in turn: "Horrible. Not great. Awful. Awful."

"Take them," I said.

"You take them. I don't want them."

Sarah came over to take a look, the View-Master still in her hand. "Let me see." She examined the tiny gray[64] images and pronounced her judgment. "This one sucks. This one's cute. This one's OK." She looked at Jenny. "You look bad in this one."

"Thanks a lot!" Jen said, and slapped Sarah with the back of her hand.

---

64 The photos were black and white even though we did have color photography at that time. I'm not that old.

Sarah yelled out, "Ow!" and held her arm where she'd been struck. "God, I just meant you look better in the second one."

"But that's not what you said," Jenny replied.

Movement caught my eye. I noticed the clerk with the blue vest appear nearby, glaring at us. I guess we were being kind of loud.

Dan must have seen her, too, because he said, "Ladies and ... dork. Let's get the hell out of here."

"Finally!" Sarah said. She walked back to the display and tossed her View-Master carelessly on top.

"HEY!" The clerk exclaimed, stomping toward us. "You break that, you buy it."

"Whatever ..." Sarah said, looking down at the clerk's nametag. "... Barb."

The clerk pointed to the entrance. "OUT."

We marched toward the exit, trying not to laugh.

When we made it back to the mall, Jen said, "That's it. I am never going back in there!"

"Fine," I replied.

As my friends walked away, I carefully folded the strip of photos in half so that the still-damp images wouldn't be touching each other. I placed them in my pocket, then hurried to catch up.

Chapter Six

J enny leaned over and whispered, "I'm going to the bathroom to wash the butter and salt off my hands."

"You're going to miss the movie," I whispered back.

"Seriously, what am I gonna miss? Another car chase? Some stupid fight scene?"[65]

I tried to do my best sexy voice.[66] "Why don't you let me ...?" I took her hand in mine and tried to suck the savory grease from her finger in a way that I hoped would be more or less seductive.

She pulled her hand away. "Gross! Now I've got, like, nine greasy fingers and one with your slobber all over it."

Nearby, someone shushed us.

Jenny got up in a huff, shoving her way through the crowd.

65 Not all girls disdain these things, just as not every guy enjoys them, but, as a trend, it's pretty solid. We were watching *Above the Law* starring Steven Seagal. It's pretty bad, actually.

66 Embarrassing.

I slumped down into my seat.

What am I doing wrong?

Sarah was across from Jenny's empty spot. "Oh, too bad!" she said, sticking her bottom lip out and tilting her head in an exaggerated expression of compassion.

I flipped her off.

I still had big plans for the night, and I was really, really hoping that this unfortunate finger-licking incident wouldn't interfere with them. After Friday night movies, Jenny and I went "stargazing"[67] until her midnight curfew. Once we got to our favorite spot, I was going to tell her everything, or almost everything. I knew it was kind of a crazy idea, but once I'd decided to be honest with her, I actually felt quite a bit better and wasn't freaking out as much as I might have if I was going to try and keep it a complete secret.

I had to talk to *someone*. Apart from Jen, the only other person I could have opened up to was my older brother Bill. He might not be happy to hear my news, but he *was* my older brother and would stick by me. He was pretty cool, in general. Dan and I were good friends, but not the kind who shared our deepest feelings or anything like that. I knew that Jenny, at the very least, would be sympathetic, even if she wasn't ecstatic. The last time we had gone "stargazing," she had done some not-so-subtle hinting that she was getting close to being ready to go all the way with me. My plan was to tell her the truth, and then, when we were feeling all open and honest and together, ask her if she wanted tonight

---

67 i.e., parking and making out. I don't know who we thought we were fooling with our terrible secret code word.

to be the night.[68] And sure, my parents' car wasn't the most romantic place to get it on, but considering how far apart we lived,[69] we didn't have a lot of options.

From the beginning of our relationship, she had wanted to wait. I was OK with that. I mean, we did everything else BUT the big deed, so I didn't feel like I was missing too much. And when it came right down to it, I wanted her to be happy. If she wanted to wait, we'd wait. I didn't know the details, but I knew that she'd been through a lot with her previous boyfriend, who was kind of a jerk, and I didn't want to upset her or bring back any bad memories.

Jen reappeared, squeezing past the row of knees as she made her way back to the seat beside me. As soon as she sat down, I could smell the odor of that pink goo that passes for soap in places like movie theaters.

"All better?" I whispered.

"All better," she replied.

In a gesture of reconciliation, I reached over with my hand to hold hers. She pulled it away in disgust.

"I just washed my hands and yours are all greasy!"

"Sorry!"

"What's wrong with you?"

"SHH!!!" came a voice from behind us.

"Fuck off!" she hissed back.

Sarah raised her hand to the give the people behind us the finger.

---

68 Two things. First, it now strikes me as sheer madness that I thought this plan would work. Second, unlike Jen, I hadn't lost (or, as I liked to say, gladly thrown away) my virginity at this time.

69 I was in the suburbs, she was in the country. The trip between us took 15 minutes by car or about an hour by bike.

Dan reached over and pulled her arm down. "It won't be you that gets jumped in the parking lot by some jerk."

Sarah crossed her arms and sulked.

When the lights came up after the movie, Jen said, "Well, that sucked royally."

Dan stood and stretched. "Girls. Y'all have no taste."

"Right, it's us girls that have no taste. Guys—burping, farting, horny dirt bags—you're the ones with taste."

Dan countered her statement with a fake karate chop and a cola-powered belch.

I laughed. Everything really was back to normal.

Out in the warm spring air, under the bright lights of the movie marquee, we said our goodbyes. Jenny put on her jean jacket, which she'd taken off for the movie. We made our way to my parent's sedan.

As I started it up, she turned on the radio and began surfing for a different station.[70]

"Watch out, the tuning knob is loose," I said.

"I know, I know," she replied. After spinning it around a while, she settled on her favorite, the top-40 station.

"You feeling OK?" I asked, as we pulled out of the parking lot.

"Yeah," she said.

I couldn't quite read her mood but I decided to take a chance. "You want to go ... stargazing?"

"Sure, I guess."

"Great," I said, trying to play it cool. We headed in the

---

70 We had a deal: my choice (rock) on the way there, her choice (pop) on the way back.

direction of the industrial waterfront. A few minutes later, I pulled into our preferred location, the back of an old factory along the lakeshore. I pointed the nose of the car out toward the water.[71] It was fairly romantic, as long as you didn't look behind you. After I cut the engine, I turned the key forward a little so the radio would come on.[72]

I looked over at Jen and smiled. She smiled back.

Yes.

I leaned over and we kissed gently. She didn't seem to be reluctant or holding back, so I kissed her again, passionately. She returned the same. I leaned in close and we embraced, our upper bodies pressing tightly against one another, breathing hotly, touching lips and tongues. I kissed her neck and caught the scent of her perfume.[73]

She leaned away from me and took off her jean jacket. We came together once again, kissing. I reached under her t-shirt and felt the soft, warm skin of her stomach and chest. It was wonderful. I felt so much for her, so much love, so much desire. I wanted to kiss her forever. But I knew I had to stop. If we kept going at this rate, I was going to get too caught up in the moment. I needed to tell her *before* we went any further. Breaking the news to her

71 The selection of a proper make-out spot for you and your paramour is a tricky business. It can't be too close to your homes, but it can't be so far that the commute cuts into your make-out time. Also, it's good to have a nice view, but you don't want to be viewed yourselves. And in the back of my head was always the illogical but lingering fear that, like in a horror movie, we'd end up the victim of a crazed serial killer if we went somewhere too remote.

72 I'm 99% sure there was an INXS song playing. They were another Australian band that was popular at the time.

73 Even to this day, if I walk by someone who is wearing the same scent, I shudder with the memory of our time together.

afterwards would be a jerk move.[74] And, if all went well, which I hoped it would, we could pick up right where we left off.

As hard as it was, I broke our embrace.

Jen pulled her shirt down. "What's wrong?"

I tried to look out the windows but our body heat had fogged them up, reducing the streetlights to blurry twinkles.

I flicked off the radio. "Nothing." My hands started to shake as I got closer to telling her. My fingertips were buzzing. I took a deep breath, trying to calm myself. "But there's something I want to talk to you about."

"Shelly, I know what you're going to say and the answer is yes."

"What?"

"I know what you're going to ask. The answer is yes. I know it was hard to wait, but I needed time. And I needed to know that you were going to stick around for me.[75] You've been really great. So ..." she slipped into her sexy voice,[76] "... did you bring any protection?"

"Oh," I said.

"Didn't you?"

"Yeah, yeah, I did.[77] And that's awesome that you're ready. But that's not what I was going to talk to you about."

Her gaze intensified with curiosity and concern. "What's going on?"

"It's nothing bad," I said, trying to assure her, "it's just

---

74 Telling her beforehand may not have been the brightest idea either, but, in my defense, I *was* trying to do the right thing.

75 This is quite funny (or not), in retrospect. But I won't say why just yet.

76 Much better than mine, I assure you.

77 They gave out a bunch in health class. I'd been hoarding them for months.

something that happened. And I'm really glad you want to do it. Like, really, really glad, seriously."

"OK ..."

"All right. OK ..." Now that the time had come, the words had left my brain. "Whoa. This is, like, really hard. I haven't talked to anyone about this."

"Just say it, Shelly. You can tell me anything."

"OK, here goes..." I tried looking at her but it was too much. I turned toward the steering wheel, took in another deep breath, and let it out slowly. "A couple of days ago, I realized that I was ... that I'm, you know, like ... bisexual."

I turned to face her. From her pained expression, I could tell that she wasn't taking the news as well as I'd hoped. Silence filled the car.

When she finally spoke, it was with anger and surprise. "You're *gay*?"

"Sort of."

"How? You're all over me!"

"I'm still totally into you. I love girls, I really, really do. I just ... I guess I like a couple of guys, too.[78] But I want to be with you. You don't have anything to worry about."

Her anger rose even higher. "What the fuck, Shel? How did you just *happen* to find this out?"

"Is that really important?" I replied, hoping to dodge the question.

"Yes, it is! I'm supposed to believe you *just* turned gay last week? Omigod, give me a break!" She looked at me and

---

78 The singer Morrissey once said, "I am humasexual. I am attracted to *humans*. But, of course ... *not many*." Fabulous, right? I'm going to try and find a spot to mention his band The Smiths later.

tried to speak, but hot tears choked her voice. "Shit!" she said and buried her face in her hands. She said it again and again, repeatedly pounding her fist on the dash in her rage. Some remote part of my brain was worried about catching hell from my parents if Jen dented the car's interior, but I didn't have the courage to ask her to stop.

"Jen," I said, "it's all OK. We're still good."

"Screw you, you lying faggot!" she yelled at me.

I yelled back. "Jen! I'm not a faggot, I'm bisexual!"[79]

"Oh, shut up. That's bullshit. Saying you're bi is just what gay guys like Elton John do before they come all the way out.[80] God! I should have known." She shook her tear-stained face. "Every guy. *Every* guy I've gone out with since I was thirteen has tried to have sex me the first chance he gets. Except for you. I thought you were being, like, a gentleman, but now I get it. Every guy ..."

"That's not it at all. I still want to, you know, fuck you."[81] I tried to reassure her by putting my hand on her leg.[82]

She pushed it aside and swung her arm out toward me, striking the side of her fist on my bicep.

"Ow!" I yelped.

We sat in strained silence, both of us breathing heavily.

After a few minutes, I tried to talk to her, to reason with her. "Jenny, we can still be together," I pleaded.

She kept her face turned to the window. "Don't even speak to me."

---

79 No comment.
80 For some, especially at that time, it seemed a "safer" option.
81 Oh ... a poor choice of words. Reading this is killing me, seriously.
82 And a poor course of action.

My throat started to feel choked off. I could barely speak. "Jenny, c'mon ..."

She held her shaking palm straight up toward me. The gesture was unmistakable: there would be no more talking.

"You want me to drive you home?" I asked.

She nodded.

The trip back to her house was excruciating. She rolled down her window and spent the whole time staring out of it, sniffling occasionally, the wind whipping her hair around her face. I tried to think of what to say to make her understand, but I couldn't come up with a single thing.

To fight the unbearable stillness, I reached down and turned the radio on. Nervously, I spun through the channels, hoping to find some innocuous sound to fill the gap between us.

With one deft move, and without ever looking away from her open window, Jenny knocked my hand away, wrenched the loose tuner knob from the radio, and hurled it out into the night. She rolled the window up and rested her face against the cool glass.

I turned the radio off.

After what felt like an eternity, we reached her house. Rather than enter her driveway, I just pulled the car over to the side of the road. I wasn't sure why. Maybe I didn't want to risk waking her parents. She pushed open the passenger door and the overhead light came on, harshly illuminating the interior.

I tried to make one last attempt at reconciliation. "Jenny ..."

Coldly, she said, "Don't ever speak to me again." She launched herself out of the car and slammed the door.

As I drove away, I heard the distinct sound of a handful of gravel hitting the back of the car.

Wonderful.

Chapter Seven

I don't remember doing it but somehow I made it home. I pulled into my driveway and had just enough brains left to check the back of the car for damage. It was hard to tell in the dark but I didn't see any marks. I unlocked the front door, my whole body shaking like a broken toy.

The house was dark, my parents already in bed. I couldn't bear the idea of talking to anyone, so I left all the lights off, tracing my hand along the walls to find my way. I entered my room, closed the door and switched on the overhead light, which was just a bare bulb set into the ceiling. The shift from soft black to bright white was blinding.[83] I fell backwards onto my bed and squinted into the light.

I was completely and utterly alone. For the first time, I saw the terrible enormity of what I was facing.

---

83 Years earlier, I was playing Star Wars in my room and had broken the glass cover in my ceiling light. It never got replaced.

Jenny ... and me ... my future ... our future ... all gone ...

It was too much. I didn't even bother to fight back the tears.[84]

I woke up around three in the morning, still dressed, lying on top of the covers. I'd thrown my arm over my face to block the light, and the end of my shirtsleeve was damp from crying. I pulled myself up onto one elbow and rubbed my eyes. I switched on my bedside lamp, which actually had a shade, then heaved myself off the bed. I stepped over the papers scattered across the floor and switched off the overhead light.

I stripped down to my boxers and caught sight of myself in the long mirror behind the door. Even in the dim light of the bedside lamp, I could tell I looked like hell. I hated everything I saw. My eyes were red, my hair was sticking up, and the room behind me was an ugly mess. I was tall, awkward, gawky. I had no muscle tone, despite all my years of swimming. There was a dark mark on my arm where Jen had hit me. My skin was pale and pasty, my face puffy and mottled.

I'm a pathetic wreck.

Who could blame Jen for hating me?

I got back into bed, switched off the lamp, and curled up in the darkness. But even though I was desperate to lose myself in sleep, it wouldn't come. I tried and tried but, now that I was awake again, something had a hold of me and wouldn't let go. My mind coiled like a centipede around

---

84 The next few weeks were a tough time. I cried a lot. Now I mostly just cry in movies.

thoughts of Jen, the guy from the pool, my friends, my life ... nothing was going to be the same.

I was crazy to ever think it would.

What was it Jen had said?

"I'm supposed to believe you *just* turned gay last week?"

I hadn't thought much about it at the time, but now her question was looming over me like a giant's shadow. I was afraid to consider the answer, because some part of me knew it went deeper than I was willing to go.

First, there was that guy in the pool. There was no arguing with the fact that I'd felt attracted to him.

Then there was that janitor. I was attracted to him, too.

And before them?

I'd been telling myself that there hadn't been any others. Now, with my defenses down, thoughts that I'd always suppressed came flowing out.

Of course there had been others! I just didn't want to believe it, not until the pool, when what was inside of me took a chance and said, "Yes."

Images slid across my mind's eye ... teachers ... movie stars ... singers ... athletes ... A thousand tiny crushes I'd never quite let myself feel. I was flooded by an unstoppable, undeniable truth: As far back as I'd had feelings for girls, I'd had feelings for guys.

I stopped breathing, paralyzed, and remained like that for a few horrible seconds. I took a deep shuddering breath that hitched in my chest.

The truth I had glimpsed in the library, the truth of that funny word with the x in the middle, was now before me, immovable. This was no glitch, no mistake, no one-time thing. I *was* bisexual. I couldn't tell myself otherwise.

And at that moment, when I should have felt absolutely hopeless, a strange thing happened. I started to feel ... different. Not happy, not by a long shot, but better. What I was feeling was *relief*. The kind you get when you set down a heavy load that you've been carrying for far too long.

Somewhere in there, I fell asleep.

Swimming the next day was pretty rough. I'd barely slept and my limbs felt heavy, like wet wool. Even though I'd made some peace with myself, I was worried about Jen and what was going to happen next. I tried to immerse myself in exertion, swimming laps, burying my face in the water, or rolling over to stare at the stained boards that lined the ceiling.

I was buoyed by thoughts of my older brother Bill, who was coming the next day for his usual Sunday dinner. I hoped that I could find the time, and the courage, to talk to him. We used to be close before he moved out to study architecture at the local university. We always fought and ticked each other off and stuff like that, but we loved each other.[85] There was nothing we couldn't talk about.

Of course, that's what I thought about Jen ...

Suddenly, Rosa appeared nearby, yelling at me, "Shel, your left-hand stroke is weak!"

I know, I know, now leave me alone.

She switched me to breaststroke and quickly found

---

85 He even taught me how to slow dance, which is going above and beyond as a brother.

another flaw in my technique. "Watch out for that asymmetrical whip-kick!"

I couldn't just laugh it off as usual, or pass the time imagining what she'd look like without her suit. My heart, head, and groin just weren't into it. I excused myself and left the pool.

The change room made me feel nauseous. It was the same place, the same lockers, same concrete floor, same bad mix of odors, and the same scratched bench where *he* had sat beside me. But now it was different. Everything reminded me of him and what had happened since. How could I sit there, alone, and be reminded of the moment when we had shared that almost-kiss?

I decided to bail on the rest of class. No, more than just one class. I was done with swimming altogether.[86]

As expected, Bill came home that Sunday afternoon. We had a classic Sunday dinner of roast ham and potatoes. Mom and Dad[87] fussed over him the whole time, nagging him about getting a steady girlfriend.[88]

When dinner was over, Bill said, "I'm going outside for some air," which meant that he was going for a beer and a smoke. I'm not sure if Mom and Dad knew or just pretended not to, but they never mentioned it.

He asked me, "You wanna come along?"

---

86 You'll see that I do go back eventually, but not for a long time.

87 I seem to have left my parents out of this story, except as they are referenced incidentally, most likely because they weren't aware of what was actually happening to me at this time.

88 He had lots of girlfriends but no steady ones. He was a bit of a player in his youth, that brother of mine.

Bill didn't usually invite me out with him, so I took his offer as a good omen. Outside, I sat down with him on the deck's bottommost steps, out of sight of our parents. Bill took a swig from his bottle of beer and set it on the flagstones. He pulled a DuMaurier Light out of its pack and lit it with a cheap green lighter.

Out of the corner of his mouth, he asked, "You want one?" and shoved the pack in my direction.

"No, thanks," I replied, trying to sound casual.

"So, what's going on?" he asked

I wondered: *Is this a casual "what's-going-on?" or a tell-me-what's-really-going-on "what's-going-on?"*

"Nothing," I replied.

"Yeah, well, you seem down." Bill took a deep drag, exhaled, and then looked over at me. He was just as tall as me, but had at least fifty pounds more muscle, and even though we had the same hair, his never looked stupid like mine.[89] "What is it? Romance?"

"Sort of."

"You didn't get Jenny in trouble, did you?"

I laughed for the first time that day. "No!"

"You two break up?"

"Probably. Did Mom and Dad put you up to this?"

"Nah, but I'm a big brother. I've got super powers for this kind of stuff."

I decided it was time to tell him the truth.

"Dude," I said, "if I tell you something, you've got to promise not to freak out."

---

[89] When the genetic wheel of fortune turned, he got it all. Plus he got the normal name. I'd hate him if he wasn't such a good guy.

Bill looked a little surprised but not too suspicious. "ok."

"I've only told one other person about this and that was Jenny, and now I've got a great big bruise on my arm to show how well that went."

He nodded, indicating that he was ready for me to talk, but my mouth had dried up. I couldn't say a word.

"Don't keep me in suspense, man."

I put my hand to my throat and tried to swallow. Bill handed me his beer and I took a sip. I was never crazy about the taste but was thankful for the moisture.

"Better?" Bill asked.

"Yeah, thanks. This is just really hard."

"All right, don't worry. I won't freak out."

"I think I'm bi. Like, as in, bisexual."

He looked at me in surprise, his eyebrows raised.

"Seriously?"

"Seriously."

"You're gay?"

"Sort of. I like girls and guys."

"Did you just figure this out now?"

"Sort of. I think it was always there; I just didn't want to know."

"Shit, Shel." He took a long drag on his smoke. As he exhaled, he said, "Dad's going to hit the roof."

"Yeah. I'm not telling them yet."

"But you told Jenny, right? That's why she broke up with you?"

"She thought that I was lying. She said that saying you're bi is just what gay guys say before they come out for real."

"Yeah, I was thinking the same thing. I think that's what Elton John did. But you still like chicks, right?"

"Totally."

"Well, maybe you're not really gay. Maybe you're just going through a phase or whatever."

"I don't think so."

"Damn," he said.

"Damn," I repeated.

"Jesus Christ, Shel. This is ..." He rubbed his forehead. "... this is complicated."

"Tell me about it."

"Are you sure you have to do this?"

"I'm not 'doing' anything." I said defensively. "This is just the way I am."

"Yeah, I get that. But if you like girls, then maybe you could, I don't know, just stick with girls."

"I don't think I can shut it off like that."

"Well, you should sure as hell try, for Mom and Dad's sake, at least."

I hadn't thought too much about what would happen when my parents found out. It would be bad, I knew that much.

Bill said, "I'm not saying it's easy. Me, I go for all different kinds of girls; it doesn't mean I have to *be* with all of them."

"That's not the same. Every girl is still a girl."

He gave me a look that said: *Do you really think that's different?*

I didn't answer because I wasn't sure.

We sat in silence for a while, both of us thinking to

ourselves. Bill finished his smoke and lit another. I took one from his pack and decided to try it. I put it in my mouth and he held his flickering lighter up to the papery end.

"Don't inhale too hard or you'll choke," he warned but it was too late. I coughed up a lungful of acrid smoke.

"Cool guy," he said. He stared over the backyard, looking toward that place where the tangled brush met the soft evening sky. "OK. I'm going to tell you something that I've never told anyone else, but you got to promise not to tell anyone. Not your friends. Not Mom and Dad. NO ONE. Understand?"

A secret part of me had hoped this would happen. That I'd come out to my brother and he'd come out right back. It would be perfect.

"Just thinking about this makes we want to puke. It's totally disgusting."

So much for my little fantasy ...

He said, "Remember the house I lived in with Rob and Jamie in my second year?"

"Yeah."

"We used to have these crazy parties there. We got hammered all the time. One night, I was getting wasted and there was this totally hot chick who was partying with us, and she and I were getting friendly all night. Except I got too drunk and had to go to bed. When I came to, I realized she was in bed with me. I went to put my arm around her and then I realized that it wasn't the girl, it was this guy, this friend of Rob's. He must have snuck into my room while I was asleep."

"Holy crap. Did he ... do anything to you?"

Bill's voice lost its usual coolness. "I don't think so. But I was so drunk, I don't remember. As soon as I realized who it was, I kicked him out of the room. Later I told Rob that I didn't want him coming around anymore." Bill took a drag on his smoke. "Shel, you can't say anything about this."

"I won't."

In a voice as angry as it was sad, Bill said, "I love you, but I'll kill you if you say anything, I swear."

I nodded.

Bill leaned forward, staring at the ground, trying to get his composure back. I glanced over at him, and the bottom fell out of what little hope I had left that someone who I cared about would be okay with who I was.

After a few minutes, Bill leaned back on his elbows, stuck out his legs, and lit up a fresh smoke. He said, "Sorry if I freaked out a bit."[90]

"It's OK," I lied.

"I told you that story because maybe you're not gay or bi or whatever, maybe you just had a bad experience or something."

"No, I'm pretty sure. Nothing bad like that's ever happened to me."

"Well ... just think about Mom and Dad before you go doing anything stupid. And don't tell anyone else about it, OK?"

---

90 At the time, I was too caught up in my own problems to worry about his. Now I feel kind of bad about not being more sympathetic to him. The incident was obviously traumatic.

"Don't worry, I won't."[91]

Considering how bad it had gone with Jen and Bill, I had no plans to open my mouth about it to anyone ever again.

"Good. Because as far as I can tell, if you don't cut it out, every version of your future sucks. Plus you'll wind up with the crap beat out of you."

He put his hand on top of my head and used it to push himself up to standing, an old trick of his. He threw his cigarette butt under the deck, picked up his beer, and went inside.

I spent the rest of the evening sitting outside on the step, thinking about everything he'd said.

---

91 Ack! Cruel irony.

Chapter Eight

A fter Bill left that night, I stared at the phone,[92] trying to summon the courage to call Jen and patch things up. But what would I say if she answered? What if one of her parents picked up?

Of course, there was always the chance that she was sitting in her house right now, doing exactly the same thing I was. Maybe she'd have the guts to call. I sure didn't.

As my eyes burned holes in the phone, it rang.

I grabbed at the receiver and said an urgent, "Hello?"

A low voice said, "Hey."

Dan.

"Oh, hey."

"Geez, don't sound so excited."

"Sorry."

---

92 No cell phones yet. No caller ID, no voicemail, etc. But we had moved from rotary dials to push-button phones, which we felt were pretty high tech.

"Why didn't you come out last night?"

There'd been a party but I'd ditched it.

"I dunno. I didn't feel like it."

"You missed out; it was good."

"Yeah."

We weren't the kind of friends who talked about our feelings or anything like that, but he could tell something was up. "You sound like crap."

I might not have been able to hide how I felt, but I was most definitely *not* going to tell him what was really going on. Every time I'd tried had been a disaster.

"Jen and I got in a fight."

"What about?"

"Nothing. It's stupid."

"She'll get over it."

"I don't know."

"Well, you should have come out and got loaded with us. You'd feel better."

Unlikely.

"Yeah."

Dan's voice brightened. "Hey, how come people on *Scooby-Doo* always act like he's so stupid even though he can talk and open doors and stuff?"

"Yeah," I replied. "They're always, like, "Oh Scooby, you stupid idiot." Meanwhile, he'd be some kind of genius dog in real life."

"Then they put him in these scary situations and make fun of him when he freaks out."

"Plus they got him addicted to Scooby snacks just so they

can make him do whatever they want. Basically, the Scooby Gang are a bunch of animal-abusing assholes."

Dan said, "Yeah, but that redhead's hot, though."

"Oh, yeah, sure, Daphne's cute, but what about Thelma? It's always the quiet ones."

We laughed and I felt a little bit better about everything.

I did my best to play it cool as I walked to school on Monday morning, but I doubt I was fooling anyone. I kept an eye out for Jenny, hoping to maybe strike up a casual conversation to start things off. You know, not get all emotional right off the bat. But it didn't take long for me to realize that things weren't going to get better any time soon.

When I got in the doors, I saw these two guys that I sort of knew heading in my direction. I could tell they were staring at me but I didn't realize why.

"Hey," I said, as I got close.

In a feminine, lilting voice, one of them said, "Very good morning!" or something

like that. I couldn't quite tell. They laughed as they passed me.

What's so funny?

I stopped and turned to watch them walk away. They were still laughing.

The way he said "very" ... it almost sounded like they were saying something else ... something like "fairy" ...

Oh, shit.

I ran in the direction of my locker. I needed to throw my

stuff in before I talked to Jen to find out what the hell she'd done. Sure, she may have been harsh at times, and she was certainly pissed off Friday night, but I couldn't imagine her actually *trying* to wreck my life, not on purpose, anyway. When I got to my locker, I saw that the word "faggot" had been scratched into the sickly beige paint, exposing the bare metal underneath.

The letters, thin and jagged, felt like they had been cut into my own skin.

I ran toward Jen's hallway. She was the only person from my school I'd told, and now everyone knew. I was furious with her and scared for myself. Through the crowd, I could see her face in profile, staring into the dark cave of her locker. My line of sight was obscured by Sarah, who was staring at me with an intense, unreadable expression. Even with my limited view, I could tell from the way Jen's brown hair hung down over her face that she wasn't doing too well. All of my anger toward her disappeared. I wanted to run to her, to hold her. I began moving in her direction but, before I got within ten feet, Sarah hurried over to me, pushing her hands against my chest.

"You've got to leave her alone, OK?" she said quietly.

"Screw off, Sarah." I said and moved to push past her. She grabbed me by my arm.

"Shel. She really needs you to leave her alone right now. Will you please do that for her?"

I'd never heard Sarah say anything so serious before.

I shouted, "Jenny!" but she wouldn't look at me. Instead,

she began to rummage in her locker, looking for ... what? An excuse not to talk to me, I suppose. I slammed my hand on the locker beside me, swore, then stormed away.

Unable to bear the crowds in the cafeteria, I went to the Appendix[93] to eat lunch. I didn't have much of an appetite, though. I'd been chewing the same mouthful of sandwich for some time when Dan arrived. His hands were stuck in his pockets as he walked slowly toward me.

"Hey," he said.

"Hrm," I mumbled back.

"Thought you'd be here."

I didn't reply. For some reason, he was irritating me just by being there.

Dan said, "So, I, uh, guess you've heard the rumors, huh?"

"No. But I can imagine what they're saying," I snapped.

"Why don't you just laugh it off? That's what I'd do."

"So I should just be like you? That would make everything perfect?"

I knew I was being a jerk but I couldn't stop.

"That's not what I meant!" He looked confused, but I was too busy being miserable to help him out.

Silence filled the space around us until I finally asked, "What's everyone saying?"

"Um, well, I've heard a bunch of stuff."

"Like what?"

"Well, people keep coming up to me to see if it's all true;

---

93 A dead-end niche in a quiet hallway, named by Dan and me for its similarity to the body part, and used as a sometimes study area.

that's how I heard about it. It's not like I'm going out of my way to hear this crap."

"Like what?" I repeated angrily.

Reluctantly he said, "That you're a fag, I guess. Someone said that you were trying to do it with Jenny and you couldn't, so she figured out that you were queer."

I laughed bitterly at that.

"But I told them it was all bull. You've got nothing to worry about, man."

"I've got all kinds of stuff to worry about."

Dan's face clouded over. "Damn, man, it's not true, is it?"

"It's part true. Enough to ruin my stupid life."

"So you, like, couldn't get it up or something? That happens to guys all the time. I heard, anyway."

"Don't act so stupid. You know what I'm talking about!"

"No, I don't! Why are you acting like such an asshole?"

"Because my life is over and you're acting like it's no big deal!"

I looked down at the floor's pale and gritty surface. My eyes began to blur with tears and I squeezed them shut. My throat felt like it was closing up. Dan sat down beside me.

"Tell me what's going on, man."

I collapsed on his shoulder, not caring if anyone saw me this close to another guy.[94]

A few minutes later, I was all cried out. And then, even though I'd sworn just the day before that I never would, I explained the story to him. Or some of it, anyway.

---

94 And not considering the risk he was taking.

"You get it?" I asked.

"I think so. You still like girls but you also like some guys."

"Yeah," I said, my voice still a little shaky.

"But that *doesn't* make you gay?" I could tell that his question was genuine, even if it sounded sarcastic.

"I used to think it didn't, but I don't even know anymore. I guess it does, sort of. Maybe being bi is different. I haven't figured it all out yet."

He seemed to consider what I'd said. "Who have you told?" he asked.

"Just you, and Jen, and my brother."

"Bill? How'd that go?"

When I first had the idea to tell someone, I thought Jen and Bill would have been the ones who understood, and that Dan would be the one to freak. Now I could see how wrong I'd been.

I said, "You're taking this way better than anyone else."

He exhaled deeply, running the fingers of both hands through his hair. "Damn, man." He looked over at me. "Maybe you can just say it was all bull and everyone will forget about it. You'll catch hell for a while but people will forget eventually, right?"[95]

"I think it's too late for that."

"But ... the assholes at this school ... they're gonna kill you."

"I know."

---

95 Don't think I hadn't thought about it.

Chapter Nine

I was sitting in a bathroom stall, feeling miserable and trying to get the courage up to face another class.[96]

I'd spent two days alternating between being furious at Jen for blabbing my secret, and then feeling terrible for upsetting her in the first place. My every effort at contacting her had been met with silence. She turned away when she saw me coming down the hall. She wouldn't answer the phone. Worst of all, she looked terrible, which made it hard to stay mad at her. I felt helpless and hopeless.

The night before, in absolute desperation, I tried calling Sarah. I was surprised that she even spoke to me.

I asked her, "What's going on with Jen? How is she doing?"

Angrily, she said, "Terrible, thanks to you."

---

96 Privacy is in short supply in any school. Bathroom stalls, as unglamorous, filthy, and malodorous as they may be, are often the only choice for someone wishing to be alone. But you probably already know that.

It was my worst fear confirmed.

"What can I do for her?"

"You can fuck off and die. Like, literally."

She hung up.[97]

Dan, on the other hand, was still friendly to me, at least on the surface. He'd say "hi" when we met but his calls had stopped. Who could blame him? I wasn't exactly a joy to be around, and gossipy whispers followed me wherever I went. What conversations he and I had were filled with awkward silences. I had taken to eating every lunch in the Appendix, just so I didn't have to talk to anyone.

I heard the door to the bathroom open and close a few times but didn't think anything of it. The bell for the next period rang with its harsh insect buzz, the noise amplified by the tiled walls and cramped space. I got myself together, shouldered my knapsack,[98] and went out into the bathroom proper. There were about six guys standing around the periphery of the bathroom. I didn't really know them but they were all staring at me.

Crap.

They wore jeans and hoodies, a kind of nondescript uniform. They didn't say anything, but it was clear from their smirking faces and menacing stances that they were waiting for me. They didn't make any moves but I knew I was in deep, deep trouble.

My eyes flicked from the guys to the door and back again. They weren't blocking the exit, but there was no

---

97 That was the last time I had any kind of conversation with her.
98 I had given up on using my locker after that first day and now carried my knapsack everywhere.

way they were going to let me just walk out of there untouched. I knew I couldn't fight my way out. There were too many of them, and I'd never been in a fight in my whole life.[99]

They grinned and stared, waiting for me to make the first move. I tried desperately to think of some way out of there that wouldn't involve losing any teeth. If only I was cooler or tougher, I could stare them down, tell them all to go to hell, but I wasn't any of those things. Out of force of habit more than anything else, I walked toward the sink. I avoided all eye contact, knowing instinctively that it would set them off. Slowly, carefully, I turned on the taps. I squirted some pink soap on my hands and rubbed them together under the warm water. When I glanced in the mirror, I could see the guys behind me. They were clearly enjoying my discomfort.

Part of me wanted them to just get it over with.

Call me a faggot, beat me up, do whatever you have to do, then just leave me alone.

I turned off the taps and moved toward the paper towel dispenser. As I got close to it, one of the guys moved to block my way. I tried to reach around him but, when I did, he leaned in close to me and burped a foul blast into my face. It reeked like a rotten can of Coke.[100] They all laughed. I wiped my hands on my jeans and moved toward the door. I kept my gaze on the floor but did my best to survey the whole room surreptitiously.

---

99 Video games don't count.

100 I don't think Coke can actually rot, but that's the closest I can come to describing it.

As I walked past one of the guys, he made a sucking, kissing sound. I didn't see it but I definitely heard it. They all must have thought this was hilarious because soon they were all doing it.

It was a straight line from where I stood to the exit, with only one guy in the way. He followed me as I walked to the door. As I reached out to open it, he slammed his hand on the metal door, making a loud bang. I flinched. In a surprising move, he reached down to the handle and pulled the door open for me. Cautiously, knowing it had to be some kind of ploy, I moved slowly toward the open doorway. As I walked through, I felt a wet thwack on the back of my head. I reached up, touched something slimy, and brought my hand back to see what it was.

A thick, filmy mucus of white and putrid green covered the tips of my fingers. It was phlegm.

I turned back to the bathroom, too humiliated and angry to worry about not infuriating them further. They didn't attack me; they didn't yell; they didn't even look me in the eye. Instead, they all just looked up toward the ceiling in exaggerated gestures, as if they were wondering, "Where did that come from?"

I stormed off, trying to think of a place where I could go to rinse my hair and wash my hand, but I was too afraid to go into a different bathroom. What if they followed me? There was nowhere to go. Right then, I realized I would never feel safe in my school again.

The Bastards,[101] as I came to call them, had decided that the best way to punish me for being myself was to make that sucking, kissing noise whenever they saw me. If I walked through a crowded hall, it was there. If I ventured into the cafeteria, as I rarely did, it was there. As I left school for my daily march home, it was there. My gut would clench as I approached them, and it would stay knotted as I stomped through their hateful gauntlet. I wanted to turn, to lash out, to strike them in their smirking faces, eternally shaded by baseball hats or hoods, but I never did.

I just kept walking.

I walked past them in the same way that I walked through my life. I ate. I slept. I went to class. I watched TV. I looked like I was awake but in actual fact I was sleepwalking through life with no clue how to wake up or get out. After a while, the terrible flow of days became a gray smear.

---

101 I don't know why I chose that particular word to describe them, but I capitalize it because these guys operated like one person. They're certainly villains in this particular story, yet I never even recorded their names. Who were they really? Did they have families and lives and loves and stories as crazy (or crazier) than mine? Certainly. But to me, they were just the Bastards.

Part Two

Chapter Ten

A few weeks after I'd gagged on the first cigarette Bill offered, he gave me another one. This time I didn't choke, but I didn't exactly love it either. Still, it seemed like something to do, something to occupy my mind, so I kept trying.[102]

We were out on the back steps again, enjoying the sunset. The weather was slightly warmer, the evenings just that much longer. Bill was nearing the end of his final semester and looking forward to finishing his degree. For my part, I just couldn't wait for summer and the chance to be free of school.

He asked, "Any improvements in your situation?"

"No," I replied. By this point, I was fully settled into my

---

102 Later, I would often use cigarettes to calm myself down. But seriously, they're terrible for you.

new "loner" routine.

"If people are pushing you around, you've got to tell the school."

I hadn't told anyone because nothing could be done about it. Sure, I could tell the school, but then what? I'd be a rat. And I'd just get it worse later.[103]

"I'm fine."

"What about your friends? They'll stick up for you."

I just shrugged.

"Come on. How long have you and Dan been friends? Like, ten years?"

"Thirteen."

"See? You can't just let that go."

I didn't tell him how far Dan and I had drifted apart.

Bill stubbed out his cigarette on a paving stone.

"Shel, I know you feel like your life sucks, but this whole woe-is-me shtick is getting old. If you can't make up with your old friends, then at least get some new ones."

"Right," I said, with as much sarcasm as I could muster. "Like that's going to happen."

The next day at school, I was staring blankly at the closed door of my locker, painfully aware of a bad smell in the area, and quite certain that it was the source. As I stood there, trying to work up the courage to crack the combination lock, someone rather small and strange appeared beside me. Although she was at least a year younger than me, I recognized her from around school because she always

---

103 I'd say that this is either-or thinking again. There were more options than this.

wore a men's tie.[104] I don't know if her grandfather knew that she was raiding his wardrobe, but she also had on a vintage man's dress shirt and suit vest. From the waist down, she was a little more traditional, jeans and black leather shoes. I don't know if it was her outfit, or the furtive way she scanned the area around us, but she looked like a miniature version of a guy in a spy movie.

"We've been coming by your locker but you're never here," she said.

Who's we? I wondered, *and why did they care?*

When I didn't reply, she blurted out, "You should come to Mr. Aiden's classroom

at lunch."

I turned back to my locker. I'd had enough crap from my fellow students. I didn't need any more.

"Seriously, you should come," she repeated, grabbing my sleeve. I looked back at her and she let go. She hustled toward another girl who was standing a few paces away. She was equally small but dressed very plainly, as if she didn't want to stand out. I didn't recognize her.

The two girls stood at the corner and conferred in hushed tones. Then the first girl, the one with the tie, hustled back to me and whispered, "Room 115," before running back to her friend. The pair took one last glance in my direction and then disappeared from view.

That was weird …

I repeated the details to myself: *Mr. Aiden, lunch, Room 115.*

---

104 Not a popular fashion of the time, but I'd seen some university girls rock the look around town.

I looked back to the empty space where the two girls had stood.

Who were they?

What happened in Room 115?

And what do I have to lose?[105]

Later that day, as casually and coolly as I knew how, I took a bathroom break from English class and cruised by Room 115. Peeking through the narrow, vertical window, I caught a glimpse of Mr. Aiden. I'd seen him before—the school wasn't that big after all—but I never knew his name.

Although he was sitting at his desk, concentrating on a pile of papers in front of him, I could see that he was tall and slim. He had a Mediterranean complexion, with short dark hair and a neatly trimmed goatee. He wore gold-rimmed glasses, a short-sleeved, buttoned-down shirt, and a tie.

Kinda square, I thought, *but handsome in his own way.*[106]

He must have felt me staring at him, because he turned his head toward me. I ducked out of sight and hustled to the bathroom.[107]

That night, I sat on my bed, propped up on a pillow, staring at the strip of photos Jen and I had taken on our final night as a couple. It was really the last time I could remember being happy. Even though it'd only been a few weeks since we'd gone into that booth, the photos felt like an ancient

---

105 Not much.

106 It's worth noting, I think, that not so long before, I wouldn't have even let myself have this thought.

107 There was one next to the sick room, which was right beside the main office. I figured it was the safest choice and so adopted it as my own.

artifact, a relic of a lost time.

My eyes ran over them again and again.

Dark blur, smiling, serious, kiss.

Dark blur, smiling, serious, kiss.

Dark blur, smiling, serious ...

The phone rang. A voice from the living room shouted that it was for me. It had been so long since I'd received a phone call, I could hardly believe it.

I picked up the receiver. "Hello?"

"Hey," Dan replied.

"Oh, hey."

"How's it going?"

Terrible.

"All right."

"Cool. Um ... I just thought you'd want to know, Jenny hasn't been at school for a few days."

In the past, she couldn't have missed five minutes of school without me knowing. Now, I was so caught up in being alone, I hadn't even noticed. I realized that I hadn't seen her since the previous week.

"What's going on?" I asked.

"I don't know. Just thought you'd want to know."

"Yeah, thanks."

"No problem."

I asked, "How's it going?"

"It's all right," he replied flatly.

There was a long moment of awkward silence.

I tried to think of something to say, some cartoon to riff on, but before I could, Dan said, "See ya," and hung up.

Five minutes later, I was in my parents' car, speeding toward Jen's house.

I knew she didn't want to see me or talk to me. And I knew that her parents would probably not want me anywhere near her, but I needed to see her.[108]

I made my way out of the suburbs, down the main roads and out into the country lanes. My headlights zoomed over the tall grasses and prickly green needles of pine trees. When I pulled onto her road, I cut the headlights.[109] The road was almost completely black. I slowed to a crawl, making my way to her house through a combination of moonlight, memory, and luck. The gravel crunched under the tires as I cruised to a stop. I got out as quietly as I could, then peered over the top of the car.

As luck would have it, there she was, framed by the large picture window in their living room. She was lying on the couch, curled up under a blanket and bathed in the electric blue glow[110] of an unseen television screen.

Is she sick?

Sad?

Or just tired?

I couldn't tell.

I felt helpless, watching her from the darkness. I considered moving closer, maybe tapping on the glass. But what good would it do?

None.

I stared for a bit longer, until an exterior light came on

---

108 OK, I know this makes me look like a weirdo, but I swear I was just concerned.

109 You could do that in the days before daytime running lights.

110 A side effect of cathode ray tube televisions. You don't get that with flat screens.

near the front door. Afraid of being caught, I started the car, crept it forward until I was past her house, then headed home.

I turned on the stereo, looking for some song to take my mind off of things. Thanks to Jen tossing the knob out the window on the night we broke up, all that was left of the tuner controls was a short metal post that was almost impossible to manipulate. I gave up and shut off the stereo. My drive home was long and silent.

As the Bastards passed me in the hall during lunch the next day, I felt something flick against my cheek. Whatever it was fell to the ground with a metallic tinkle. I looked down and saw a penny skip across the floor. A half-second later, another coin bounced off the back of my head. Several more struck my back and I hurried away, leaving the Bastards to snicker behind me as I left.

Whatever's waiting for me in Room 115 can't be any worse than this.

I walked to Mr. Aiden's classroom and stood by the door. I took a breath, pushed open the door, and went in.

The first thing I noticed was that it was darker inside, the overhead fluorescent lights switched off. I liked that. Otherwise, it was a typical classroom. Textbooks sat on a low shelf under the chalkboard. History posters covered the walls.

The girl with the tie and her partner-in-crime were already there, along with Mr. Aiden. There was a rather odd-looking guy sitting in the back, with unruly hair and thick, owlish glasses. I thought maybe I'd seen him around. He was working at the back of the room on a computer.111 Next to Mr. Aiden was a guy about my own age, wearing stylishly ripped jeans and tortoiseshell sunglasses. He was staring out the window, his lips pursed thoughtfully. Him I *definitely* didn't recognize. He didn't go to our school, I knew that for sure.

"Hi," I said to no one in particular.

When he heard my voice, Mr. Aiden looked up from his work. "Hi, you must be Sheldon. Come on in, have a seat."

He gestured to a desk and chair.

In a soft, high voice, the partner-in-crime said, "This is the lunchtime study club."

I must have looked lost because Mr. Aiden said, "It's not an official club. Just an informal thing."

I sat down in the offered chair, setting my knapsack beside me. I had an inkling of what this place was. That girl with the boyish clothes, the stylish guy, and now me. Not everyone in the room could be pegged as gay or bi right away. I certainly didn't think that I could, but who said we all had to fit someone else's idea of what we should look like?

And what about Mr. Aiden? Is he gay, too?

The thought of being with other people like me was as thrilling as it was terrifying.

Mr. Aiden's voice was calm. "This is just a quiet place for students to come and have lunch. Students who maybe don't have anywhere else they feel comfortable."

---

111 Probably a TRS-80. Compared to your average computer of today, it had the processing power of one of those batteries you make out of a potato.

The stylish guy looked at me and said, "It's the homo club."

Homo club?

Calmly, but with obvious irritation, Mr. Aiden said, "Andrew, I've talked to you about ..."

"I know. I'm on probation." Frowning, he held out his wrists as if waiting for some invisible handcuffs.

Andrew may not have been flamingly feminine, but my instincts[112] told me that he was indeed a homo, a queer, a faggot ... all of those words I'd read in the Library, heard in the halls, and even said myself. And he didn't seem to care. He was so confident, so scary in his own way, I felt like I was in a cage with a lion.

Mr. Aiden stood up. "I think introductions are in order. This is Andrew ..."

"I'm changing my name to Prince Adam of Eternia,"[113] Andrew replied nonchalantly.

"Well, you're Andrew for now. And this is Mary-Beth." He gestured to the partner-in-crime. "And I believe you've already met Marta."

"Also known as the mini-dykes," Andrew said with a snort.

Marta looked to Mr. Aiden who gave her a conciliatory look.

"Andrew, behave yourself and respect your fellow students or your privileges here will be revoked. I'm serious." He turned back toward me. "I taught Andrew at my last school, and he's doing independent coursework here *provided* he

---

112 AKA"gaydar"—that intuitive sense that lets LGBTQ people identify each other. It's magic!

113 From the muscle-bound hero of He-Man cartoons.

follows the rules of his probation, which include showing up on time and showing respect for students and staff."

Andrew's only reply was a bored wave.

"And back there is Tim." He raised his voice and called out, "Tim, can you come up here a minute?" Like a startled bird, Tim turned his head toward us. The Coke-bottle glasses he wore added to his look of general bafflement. He stared at us for a moment with magnified eyes and then, without a word, he turned back to the computer and resumed typing.

"Being a fairy is the least of his problems," Andrew said. I could tell that he was only partly joking.

"Andrew!" Mr. Aiden said in exasperation. "Shel, would you like to introduce yourself?"

"Uh, OK. Well, my name is Sheldon Bates and I'm in Grade 12. That's about it."

Andrew said, "And ... you're a homo. Welcome to Homo Club."

This is it, I thought. *This is the moment. I say what's in my heart and just maybe stop feeling so alone. Then again, I'd be tripling the number of people I've told. And I'd be telling a whole group ...*

There would be no going back after this, not ever.

With every ounce of quaking courage I could muster, I pronounced, "I'm actually bisexual."

Andrew let loose an explosion of laughter.

"Andrew ..." Mr. Aiden warned.

"How nice to have a fence-sitter[114] in our little group! How long do you think that'll last?"

---

114 A derogatory term for bi people, as if we're bi because we can't choose one or the other. Lame.

"Andrew, for the last time ..."

"Oh, Darren," he said, using the teacher's first name like an insult, "you know he's full of it. It's always just a matter of time."[115]

Mr. Aiden pointed to the door. "Andrew, Office. Now. Go."

"All right, but that's the end of my probation. I guess I'll just ..."

"Fine. Go to ..." Mr. Aiden squeezed his eyes shut, then opened them again. "... Go to the Guidance Office. Stay there until next period."

"Ciao, all," he said. Looking right at me, he added, "Bye, Switch."[116]

He gathered his coat, swept it over his shoulder with a flourish, and strolled out of the room.

"I'm sorry about that, Sheldon. Andrew needs to improve his social skills. I want this to be a place where you can come and feel safe.[117] Andrew ... well ... he's been through a lot, and I'm trying to help him out ... but he doesn't make it easy at times."

"Like, all the time," said Marta angrily.

"I apologize to all of you on his behalf." Mr. Aiden looked at me and said, "I know it took a lot to open up to us like that. You shouldn't have to deal with his negativity."

I said, "I've heard worse."

A smile, small and slightly sad, crossed his face. "Well,

---

115 See also: Jen's Elton John comment.

116 Short for switch-hitter, another term for bisexuality, although not a particularly derogatory one. Either way, my soon-to-be, rarely-used, and short-lived nickname was born.

117 I think it's important to note here just how far out on a limb Mr. Aiden was going for us. There were no gay/straight alliances at this time, and any teacher who attempted to run a covert one probably risked losing his or her job.

now you're free to just have your lunch in peace if you like."

Everyone settled down and went back to what they were doing. I grabbed my lunch and, for the first time in ages, ate it in relative comfort.

When the bell rang, we said goodbye and headed to our classes. I had a spare, so I walked toward the library, thinking of the lunchtime study group and Mr. Aiden in particular.

I felt happier than I had in ages. As I walked home at the end of the day, I passed Duncan mowing his lawn. He was wearing a baseball cap, heavy metal T-shirt, cut-off jean shorts, and running shoes without socks. I mimed saying, "How's it going?" and even gave him a friendly wave.

Hi, Duncan! Even you and your surly stares can't bring me down right now!

He gave me a barely perceptible nod of his dark, shaggy head and continued mowing.

Chapter Eleven

———

Dan sat down beside me in Mrs. Piedmont's English class. We said "Hey" to each other, but no more. The gulf between us seemed too big to cross.

Mrs. Piedmont began handing back our latest assignment. I got a B, which was higher than I expected and probably more than I deserved. I had pretty much stopped trying. If things kept going as they were, I'd be lucky to wind up with a C by the end of the semester.

The assignments returned, she cut short the class's general grumbling with another one of her boring lectures, all of which sounded like they were being read from some invisible prepared script.[118]

———

118 In retrospect, I realize what a thoughtful and intelligent teacher she was. I didn't appreciate it at the time. Anyway, this class was pretty much the starting point for a whole lot of stuff that's about to happen. I didn't know that at the time, so I wasn't paying any particular attention and therefore I can't say that this is 100% word-for-word, but I did keep the handout she gave us, so I know I have the

"Speech writing is an ancient and important art, one that each of you should be able to master. Countries and kingdoms have fallen or prospered on the strength of their orators. Cicero, Churchill, Kennedy, these are the speakers who have earned a place in history ..."

Blah blah blah ...

My mind was a million miles away, thinking of Jen, the kids in Mr. Aiden's room, and the man himself.

My mind spun around and around, eventually coming back, as it often did, to that guy in the swimming pool, the moment our lips touched, the moment when he breathed for both of us. I knew that I should have kept up with my swimming[119] but I couldn't bear returning. I thought of him and that one class we had together, and what could have happened if we'd just had a little more time ...

My reverie was cut short by the sound of rustling papers. I looked around. Most of my classmates were reading from a sheet of paper. I was wondered where mine was and then I realized I was holding it in my hand. At the top it said "ENG4AO, Speech Writing."[120]

Mrs. Piedmont continued. "Over the next two weeks, you will be working on speech writing and public speaking. Many of you are no doubt displeased to hear this, but I assure you, these are skills that will serve you well. Please follow along on your handout as I go through each item."

She went through the sheet of paper, checking off the steps for a good speech: select, research, organize, first

---

points right, and I do think I managed to capture her particular way of speaking.
119 Exercise is like magic for improving my mental state, but I don't feel like doing it when I'm down.
120 I told you I kept the handout.

draft, practice, revise, memorize, present. The usual stuff.

"If you follow each of those steps, I can almost guarantee you an excellent mark. However, experience has taught me that most of you will *not* follow those steps and your mark will suffer accordingly. I've also learned that people tend to develop sudden illnesses on the day their speech is due. If you are not in class on your day, I will need a doctor's note and you will *still* need to complete your speech when you return."

Like I said, she was old school.

Certain that many of my classmates hated me, I was terrified at the thought of standing up in front of them.

"Speeches will be evaluated as follows: Quality of text, 50%; quality of presentation, also 50%. Remember that *how* you present your speech is as important as *what* you present. Now, flip over the page."

On cue, we flipped over our papers, filling the room with a soft swishing sound.

"As I said, the class will judge the speaker. This is important because, unlike an essay, a speech must not only be well written, but must also be appreciated by its audience. I will select the winner based on a combination of the class's opinion and my own.

We grade each other? She may as well just fail me now.

"The winning speaker will go on to the school finals against the other Grade 12 classes. It should be noted that my class has been the reigning champion for the past seven years, and I'd like to continue our winning streak. The top entry from the school will then participate in the city finals, where the best orator from each school in the Board will compete for the grand prize. I hope to see some excellent work from you.

"Now, on to Suggested Topics. Almost any subject—I emphasize the word *almost*—is suitable. Past winning topics have included "Today's Teenager," "How My Family Came to Canada," and "My Favorite Historical Figure.""

Kelly, one of my classmates put her hand up, something she did numerous times each class.

With the faintest hint of exasperation, the teacher said, "Yes, Kelly?"

"I won the school public speaking finals at my elementary school."

Several members of the class let out an audible groan.

Mrs. Piedmont was gracious in her response. "Well, congratulations. We'll expect big things from you."

"My topic was 'Stickers.'"

"Lovely," said Mrs. Piedmont, terminating the conversation.

Chapter Twelve

The next day as I was heading back to Mr. Aiden's class, I bumped into Dan. He said, "Hey. How's it going?"

"Good," I replied.

"Cool. Where you headed?"

"Room 115."

"Why?"

I shrugged. "Just to study."

"Oh."

Before the awkward silence grew too big, I said, "I gotta go."

Dan gave me a little wave of his hand as I turned and walked away.

I felt like crap. I knew he was struggling, and I knew I wasn't helping him with it, but I didn't feel like we were even on the same planet anymore. How was I supposed to relate to anyone from my old life? And I couldn't tell him where I was going, not without explaining why I was going there. Room 115 had to stay a secret, for the sake of everyone involved.

I hurried to Mr. Aiden's room. Now that I had some place to go to feel safe, I felt like the rest of my life was spent holding my breath. Once inside his shaded classroom, I could finally breathe again.

Mr. Aiden greeted me casually.

"Hi Sheldon. Good to see you again."

"Hi."

Spending time with Mr. Aiden was a large part of the appeal of Room 115. I was starting to admire everything about him, from his slim, muscular physique to his slightly dorky sense of style.

Marta and Mary-Beth were there, focused on a large book that was spread out in front of them. They said "Hi," then went back to their reading. Tim was at the back, in what I would come to know as his usual spot, working on the computer.

What's he do back there? Homework?

I had mixed feelings when I saw that Andrew was absent. I was kind of fascinated by him, with his confidence, style, and secretive ways. But he was unpredictable, too; you never knew when he was going to lash out in some way.

I set my knapsack down and tried to sneak a peek at the book the girls were reading. I couldn't make it out clearly, but it sure looked gay from where I was standing. I didn't know where they'd get something like that. Certainly not in the school library.

Mr. Aiden said, "If you like, we have more books in that cupboard."[121] He gestured toward a small, nondescript cabinet pushed up against the wall. It certainly didn't look like it held anything of interest, but I suppose that was intentional.

I walked over to the cupboard, squatted down, and pulled open the doors. Inside were some small cardboard boxes. I opened them up and looked inside. Their contents were a revelation: a treasure trove of books, magazines, and pamphlets on gays and lesbians.[122] Nothing explicit, nothing that would get you kicked out of school for having, but stuff you might not want other people to see you with.

I pulled out a single-volume encyclopedia of sorts. The title said that it was about "queer"[123] history. Straightaway, I looked up bisexuality in the index[124] and was ecstatic to see an entire chapter dedicated to the topic. I scanned it quickly to get a sense of what it had to say. There was a section on myths about bisexuality, like how everyone thinks it's just a phase, or how we want to have sex with everyone. There was a bit about how your sexuality can change over the course of your life, which I'd never heard of, but which made sense.

What really fascinated me was a list of famous people

---

121 This was classic Aiden, encouraging and vague at the same time.

122 I cringe mentally at how out of date the material in there would now seem, but it was all we had. Note the use of the terms "lesbians" and "gays" but no others. More on that later.

123 My first experience with LGBTQ re-appropriation, i.e., taking something bad (an insult) and reclaiming it as something of our own. It seemed really weird to me but I got used to it quickly.

124 Old habits die hard, I guess.

who loved both guys and girls. I couldn't believe there were so many. These were people just like me, but they weren't freaks or outcasts, they were amazing people living incredible lives. They were *in* the world, not just slinking around in the shadows. It was unbelievable. I flipped through pages, looking at their portraits, reading their stories. I didn't know who most of them were, but I traced my finger over their names, saying them in a whisper, like an incantation.

Sappho, Cocteau, Diaghilev, Nin ...

I read and read until the bell rang for next period. I hadn't even had a bite of my lunch, but I could eat it on my spare. I thought about asking if I could take the book with me, but somehow I knew that the books had to stay in Room 115.

Wishing I didn't have to leave, I gathered up my knapsack, said goodbye, and headed to the library, already looking forward to the time when I'd return.

And I did return, the very next day.

And the day after that.

And the day after that.

Mr. Aiden's class became the center of my universe. Every lunch period would find me rummaging through the cupboard, chomping on a sandwich, and digging like a starving dog into some book or other.

As for the other kids in the class, well, we may have been all together in one room, but we weren't friends—not yet, anyway. Tie-wearing Marta and silent Mary-Beth, that inscrutable, inseparable pair, kept to themselves. As for Tim, he barely seemed to be on the same planet as the rest of us. Andrew came and went, his moods unpredictable, but usually bad.

But Mr. Aiden, he was *always* there. He never talked about himself or his personal life; that was clearly off limits. We didn't know if he was actually gay.[125] But when I walked into his classroom, I felt safe. I came to love the smell of his cologne[126] and his friendly smile. My crush continued to grow. I became obsessed with the way the dark hair on his forearms contrasted with the light color of his shirtsleeves. I'd catch myself staring and have to shake my head to snap out of it.[127]

I couldn't make my life go back to the way it was, but I finally felt like I had a real chance to make a new one.[128]

---

125 Anything else seemed unlikely, but you know what they say about assuming. p.s. He was gay.

126 I still smell it on someone from time to time. Takes me back.

127 If you're worried about getting caught staring at a body part, forearms are a pretty safe choice.

128 I didn't want to interrupt myself earlier because I thought I was having a nice moment, but in case you're wondering, Sappho was an ancient Greek poet, Jean Cocteau was an artistic multi-threat, Sergei Diaghilev founded the Russian Ballet, and Anais Nin was, amongst other things, a famous diarist.

Chapter Thirteen

I was wandering around the mall, waiting for my parents. I hit the usual stops, like the bookstore and the music shop. I even went back to that dingy department store I'd dragged everyone into. I knew no one who worked there would recognize me or remember that I'd been kicked out. The place was so empty it looked abandoned. I poked around for a while, the sole shopper, looking at this and that. I went to the rear of the store and its wall of creepy aquariums. A lot of the fish were drifting belly up in the water. I guess no one working there really cared enough to clean the dead ones out. I saw the old photo booth, sitting unused in the half-light, the heavy dark curtain masking its dark interior. I couldn't imagine going back into it ever again. In the food aisle, I found that jar of ghostly pickled onions floating around in murky brine.

None of it seemed funny anymore.

What was different? Had the store changed or had I? Whatever the reason, being there was bringing me down, so I made for the exit.

As I headed out, I spied Dan walking toward me. For a moment, I thought about ducking out on him but he was too close.

"Hey, man," I said.

"Oh, hey," he replied.

"What's going on?" I tried to sound casual, like us meeting up was no big deal.

He shrugged. "Nothing. Just waiting for my mom."

"Me too."

He hooked his thumb in the direction of the food court. "I'm going to get some fries."

I took it as an invitation. "Cool," I said and we began to walk. Jen had returned to school, but I hadn't yet learned why she'd been off. I wanted to ask him about it but I didn't think we were quite there yet.

We began to chat, just small talk, movies, TV, school, cars. (No girls, not yet.) We rarely agreed on specifics when it came to any of those things, but we shared the same interests. He began talking government politics, something he always had a greater interest in than me. I wasn't really listening, to be honest. Our conversation was a little strained, but it felt cool to be hanging out again.

As we sat down with our fries and Cokes, I finally got the courage to ask, "Have you heard any more about Jen?"

"No," he replied, keeping his eyes on his fries. "She's

back now. I haven't seen her much, anyway. Without you around, we don't really have a reason to hang out."

"Sure, yeah. What about Sarah?"

"What *about* Sarah?" Dan said, stuffing his mouth with a handful of fries, ketchup covering them like thick blood.

"Well, you guys are still, y'know, 'friends,' right?"

"God, how many times do I have to tell you that there's nothing going on?"

"Jeez, sorry. I was just asking."

"Well, there's nothing to say about it. I see her around sometimes, that's it. We're not even really friends anymore."

I wanted to ask him more about that but it didn't seem like a wise thing to do.

"OK, all right. Sorry."

Dan didn't reply. The tension was agonizing.

I finally said, "This sucks."

"I know," he admitted.

"We're supposed to be buds."

"Well, I'm not the one who changed!"

Part of me wanted to smack him for that, for making me the sole reason that everything went so wrong. But another part of me felt that he was totally right, and I just didn't want to admit it.

Dan got up and emptied his tray into the garbage. I followed suit.

We stood beside the garbage pails for a while, not talking or making eye contact. Eventually I asked him, "You wanna go to the record store?"[129]

---

129 Like I said earlier, we used to buy our music as physical objects. It was all LP's or cassettes at the time.

"Sure," he replied.

After we had walked a bit, Dan said, "You know, if you want to know how Jenny is, you should just talk to her."

"I tried, but she won't talk to me. She hates me."

"She was just upset. You should try again."

"You think so?"

"She's had some time to cool down. I think she might want to hear from you."

"How do you know?"

"I don't know, it just makes sense, that's all. You know how girls are. They're all crazy with hormones and stuff."

I pondered his suggestion as we walked.

Maybe he's right. Maybe she would talk to me now. And is it ridiculous to think that we might get back together? It sure would make things easier for me at school to have a girlfriend again. And we were about to do it, too ...

Then I remembered that first day when all hell broke loose.

It's Jen's fault everyone knows. I'm the one who should be mad at her!

"I'm still kind of pissed at her, too, though," I said, "Y'know, for spilling my secret and all that."

"It wasn't her that did it," Dan replied.

"What? Who did?"

"Sarah."

Sarah. It figures.

But still, she wouldn't have been able to spread a rumor if she didn't know about

it in the first place.

I said, "Yeah, but Jenny's the one who told her."

Dan raised his arms in frustration. "All I know is, Jen was really upset and so she told Sarah, but asked her not to say anything to anyone else. Then Sarah went ahead and told everyone, anyway. So, yeah. That's why I haven't seen her."

I had a sick feeling in my stomach, a terrible guilt. Dan had ditched Sarah and he'd done it for my sake. I never considered just how much all of it had affected him. I wanted to say something, to thank him, but I couldn't put the words together in a way that sounded sincere.

Instead, I said, "Sarah never said anything about it when I saw her that next day."

"No, she wouldn't."

"Dammit. Why would she do something like that?"

"Who knows why she does anything, man? Maybe she was mad at you for upsetting Jenny. Maybe she's just a total bitch."

We got to the small record store and began browsing the shelves, each in our own areas of taste. They had the usual mix you might expect in a suburban mall, mostly pop music and other mainstream stuff. It made me think of Jenny, because she and I could never agree on music. At one point, I looked up and found myself staring at a black AC/DC T-shirt pinned to the wall. My mind flashed back to the thesaurus I had covertly read way back when.

I should wear that to school! Screw all the Bastards! Everyone's heard the rumors already. Why shouldn't I wear it just to show them I don't care?

I kept staring at the shirt, the gears in my mind turning over.

Because I do care. Because it will only make things worse.

Maybe, I thought, *but maybe not.*

Dan's voice snapped me back to reality. "I've gotta split, Shel. I'm meeting my Mom down by the far end of Sears."

"I'll walk you down."

A short distance later, Dan asked, "What's with that class you've been going to at lunch?"

I wanted to tell him the truth, I really did. But I wasn't sure I was ready to. Plus, I didn't want to draw any attention to the other kids there.

"It's just Mr. Aiden's class. He's cool."

"He's the guy with the goatee?"

"Yeah."

"Is he, like, gay or something?"

Probably ...

"I don't know. He just lets me and these other kids hang out in his room. I like it there."

"Why?"

I knew it would hurt Dan but I said, "Because I feel like nobody else wants me around."

"That's bull."

"No, it isn't."

"You're just making things worse by not hanging out with anyone."

"That's easy for you to say. I'm the one who's been getting harassed by these jerks at school."

"Who?"

"I don't know, just these Bastards."

"You should, like, tell the principal or something."

"Yeah, like that would help anything."

Dan stopped at the entrance to Sears. "All right, see ya 'round."

I said, "I can walk you to the door, if you want."

"Nah, it's all right."

I wondered if he didn't want his mother to see us hanging out together.

He began to walk away but stopped after a few steps. "You should really try to talk to Jenny again," he said. "Things could ... I don't know, maybe they could go back to the way they used to be."

I said, "Yeah, maybe." But did I really believe it?

Just as he was about to walk away, I shouted, "Hey!"

He stopped and turned to face me.

I asked him, "How come Garfield hates Mondays so much? He doesn't even have a job."

He smiled and shrugged, then walked away.

It's a nice idea, a really nice idea, but things are never going back.

When he was out of sight, I headed back to the record store.

Chapter Fourteen

Tim was the last one holding cards. He threw them all down on the desk. "I hate playing this game. I'm always the stupid Janitor."[130]

"Clean 'em up, Janitor," Marta said.

Tim gathered up the pile of cards and began to shuffle. "This sucks."

"Next time, don't play all your power cards so soon,"[131] I suggested.

It had taken some time and some gentle encouragement, but I'd managed to get the kids in the lunch club to actually start talking to each other. Some days, like this one, we even played cards, which is something I missed doing with Jen, Dan, and Sarah.

---

130 "President" is the polite name (there are many others) for this card game where you try to get rid of all of your cards as fast as you can. First person out is President, then Vice-President, Secretary and, finally, Janitor.
131 Twos and Jokers, the most powerful cards in the game.

As soon as our next hand started, Tim was right back at it, throwing away his best cards, leaving nothing for the rest of the hand. After a few go-rounds, I'd played all my cards and had once again secured my position as President.

Maybe it was because I was so good at math, or maybe just because I'd played the game a million times, but I usually came out on top. Marta and Mary-Beth didn't seem to mind.

While the other three battled it out for the remaining positions, I looked around Room 115. Mr. Aiden was reading. Andrew sat a few desks over, headphones on, listening to music on his Walkman.[132] I could hear him singing softly along with the song. His voice was surprisingly high and sweet.

I elbowed Marta and gestured in Andrew's direction. She was as surprised as I was. Soon all four of us were listening in.

I don't know if it was the end of our chatter that caught his attention, but Andrew seemed to sense us watching him. He turned in our direction, pulling off his headphones.

"What?" he asked in an accusatory tone.

"Nothing," I replied.

In her quiet, bird-like way, Mary-Beth said, "You have a real nice singing voice."

He seemed to be looking for some hint of an insult, some reason to lash out at us, but there was none to be had.

---

132 The analog precursor to the iPod. It played cassettes or the radio.

He said, "Thanks," making the word sound almost like a warning.

We looked at each other, surprise spreading across our faces. It was the most polite we'd ever heard him be.

Will wonders never cease?

I asked, "What are you listening to?"

Slowly, he held up a cassette case for a band called The Communards.[133] I nodded, trying to act like I knew who they were. Andrew replaced his headphones, then turned back around.

We went back to our game.

Marta threw down her last card. "Vice," she said, and straightened her tie as a sign of victory.

Mary-Beth followed. "Secretary."

Tim tossed his remaining cards onto the desk. "I'm the stupid Janitor again."

As I walked down the hall, someone pulled on my sleeve. Expecting an attack, I flinched. None came. A girl I didn't recognize was standing right behind me. Another one stood further away. They looked around themselves nervously. I didn't recognize either of them, but they looked much younger than me.

"What?" I asked.

They didn't answer.

---

133 Late 80s dance band fronted by openly gay singer Jimmy Somerville. He has an incredible falsetto. His earlier band, The Bronski Beat, made the first clearly gay pop song I remember, "Smalltown Boy." There were other bands at the time that had special appeal to LGBTQ teens, like The Smiths, Depeche Mode, and the Pet Shop Boys, but I didn't like them (or chose not to like them) because they were all "too gay." I came around on most of them later.

"Hurry up," said the one who was further away.

"What?" I repeated, growing angry.

"You gotta watch out," the sleeve-puller said.

"Watch out for what?"

"These guys. They hate you. They're gonna pink blanket you."

"What are you talking about?"

"It's when you take a white blanket and you throw it over a queer and then pound on it till it turns red."

I was dumbfounded.

"From *blood*," she added, in case I'd missed the point.

"Why would they do that?" I asked.

"'Cause they hate you."

"Yeah, but why do they hate me?"

As if I didn't already know.

"Duh. 'Cause you're a faggot?"

"Nice. And you're friends with these guys?"

"Well, yeah," she answered, as if my question was the dumbest one in the world.

"Why?"

She shrugged. "'Cause they're cool."

The other girl began pulling on her arm, trying to get her to leave. "We gotta go," she said. They started away, but I had to ask them one more question.

"Why are you telling me?"

"'Cause they're gonna get in trouble if they do it. Don't tell anyone we told you."

"Thanks," I said as they walked away.

As they hurried away, the sleeve-puller said, "Seriously.

They already got the blanket here."

As soon as they were gone, the bell rang and the hallway filled with students. I let the crowd push me toward my next class, unable to shake the image that was forming in my mind. I could see myself half-dead, bloody, wrapped in a sheet down some darkened hallway at school.

They could do it, too.

Who could stop them?

I was feeling pretty shook up when I arrived at Mrs. Piedmont's class.

Dan said, "Hey." His tone seemed just the teensiest bit friendlier than it had before. A good sign.

Thankfully, our teacher gave us the class to work on our speeches. I wouldn't have been able to concentrate on any real work.

Dan asked me what I was going to do my speech on.

I said, "I don't know yet."

I'd learned so much in Mr. Aiden's books that I was thinking about doing it on something from there, like a famous person or something like that, but I wasn't ready to go all out, so to speak, in front of the whole class.

"Maybe some artist or something," I said.

"Cool," he replied.

I asked him what he was working on, and he held up a book with a slick-looking sports car on the cover.

"Porsche?" I asked.

He nodded.

"Right on."

I was feeling a bit better, but the thought of that bloody blanket wouldn't leave my mind.

Later, with classes over, I cracked open the exit doors near the Appendix and peered out. The coast was clear. I stepped out into the dusty air and began heading for home. The Appendix exit was on the south side of the school, as far away from home as you could get but, when I used it, I could go from one corner of the school to the other without having to walk through the halls, which meant that I had a better chance of avoiding the Bastards.

Shouldering my knapsack, I trudged along the strip of patchy grass and weeds that ran along the bottom of the windowless south wall. I rounded a corner and almost fell right on top of Jen. She was sitting on the ground with her knees pulled up and her back against the bricks. She was dressed in shorts, sunglasses, and a tight T-shirt.

I hadn't been that close to her in ages, and the passion I'd felt for her came rushing back. I guess I'd spent so long worrying about the part of me that liked guys, I'd almost forgotten how much I liked girls, especially her.

"Whoa, sorry," I said awkwardly. We hadn't spoken in weeks and here I was, literally tripping over her. She had a pen in one hand and was writing in a notepad that was resting on her smooth bare leg.

She closed the notebook. "S'okay."

She didn't seem upset or anything, just deep in thought. There was so much I wanted to say to her. I thought of what Dan had told me about Sarah's role in the whole mess, and how I should try to talk to Jen again. I decided to take a shot.

"I never saw you out here before," I said.

"I was just looking for a somewhere quiet to write."

Write? Jen had never written anything in her life that wasn't schoolwork or a note to pass in class.[134]

I said, "It's hard to find somewhere to be alone around here."

She nodded.

"You're not taking the bus home?" I asked.

"No, I'm getting a ride later."

She wasn't running away, which I thought was a good sign.

Do I press my luck?

"You want some company or anything?"

She shifted her weight, setting her notepad down on the grass and then crossing her legs. I felt my eyes being magnetically drawn to where the white material of her shorts gathered tightly around the tops of her thighs. I tried to swallow but my mouth had gone dry.

Don't stare at her crotch.

You are trying to make up with her so don't stare at her crotch.

Do something else.

Find a distraction.

Just don't stare at her crotch.[135]

"No, I think I just want to keep on writing," she said. "Maybe later."

I was disappointed but also kind of relieved. If I had to

---

134 A primitive form of texting.

135 This is good advice for just about any time and circumstance.

spend any more time trying *not* to stare at her crotch, I would eventually embarrass both of us.

"Oh, OK. I guess I'll see ya around."

"Bye. I'll call you, OK?"

It was the best news I'd heard in a while.

"Great," I replied and headed home, smiling.

Chapter Fifteen

M r. Aiden was sitting quietly at his desk. Andrew was sleeping in a chair by the window, which he often did. No one knew where Tim was. Mary-Beth, Marta, and I were huddled around a table, reading. To be honest, while I did have a book open in front of me, I wasn't actually reading it. I couldn't focus. My sandwich sat on the desk beside me, barely touched. I kept thinking about what those girls had said about the pink blanket.

Mary-Beth, whose voice never went much above a whisper, leaned over and said quietly, "Are you OK?"

I whispered back, "Yeah."

Under her breath, Marta asked, "What's going on?"

I wasn't up to spilling my guts about everything that was going on. Besides, we didn't really do that in Room 115.

"Nothing," I replied.

Marta's eyes flicked over to Andrew. She whispered, "Do you have a crush on him?"

No one had ever asked me something like that about a guy before. It was kind of shocking.

Mary-Beth said, "Marta!"

Her friend shrugged. "What?"

Andrew was attractive, there was no denying that, and he certainly knew how to dress, but I couldn't get past his abrasive personality. I shook my head.

"I just thought 'cause you're always looking at him."

I was?

I looked at Marta and whispered, "Nah." Then I decided to turn the tables. "Who do *you* have a crush on?"

"From school or anyone?"

"Anyone."

She didn't even have to think about it. "Belinda Carlisle."[136]

"She's cute," I said. I had never had this kind of conversation with anyone who was gay or bi or anything. It was a little weird but kind of fun.

I looked at Mary-Beth. "What about you, MB?"

She looked at Marta, then silently shook her head.

"She's shy about stuff like that," Marta said. "What about you?"

I wasn't ready to say any names out loud, not of guys, anyway.

"It's more than a crush, I guess, but I just talked to my ex-girlfriend for the first time in a while."

"Do you still like her?"

---

136 Former lead singer of the all-girl rock group the Go-Go's. By this time, she also had a very successful solo career.

"Yeah, a lot."

Then she asked, "Do you think you like girls or guys more?"

I hadn't really thought about it in terms of percentages.

"I'm not sure. The same, I guess."

Mary-Beth whispered, "Maybe you're pansexual."

"What's that mean?"

"I don't know. I was just reading about it."[137]

Without even opening his eyes, Andrew said, "What are you homos whispering about?"

"Andrew ..." Mr. Aiden warned.

I looked across the desk at Marta and Mary-Beth. As if we were keeping the biggest secret in the world, all three of us said "Nothing" in unison.

A faint smile crossed Andrew's face.

When the bell rang at the end of lunch, I headed to the Appendix to study, or at least try. I was walking with my head down, not looking at where I was going, when I turned a corner and strolled right into a nest of the Bastards. They began making the kissing sounds and flicking little pieces of folded paper at me. I stopped, my guts tightening and my brain boiling in anger, shame, and frustration. I kept walking, going right through them. I could hear them saying "faggot," "fairy," "homo," all the usual names they had for me.

After I'd passed by them, I could still hear their voices behind me. I stopped walking and turned to face them. They went silent, waiting to see what I would do next.

---

137 An attraction to all people regardless of sexuality or gender, as opposed to the more binary mode of bisexuality.

Very quietly, something ignited inside of me.

Maybe it was because I was feeling more confident. Maybe I was tired of living under their shadow. Or maybe my terror of the pink blanket made me snap.

I said, "Fuck you."

They came at me like a pack of wolves. I dropped my knapsack and fled. I tore through the back hall, running as fast as I could.

I skidded around a corner, pushed open a metal door and took stairs four at a time up to the next level. The second floor hall was a straight stretch. Classroom doors flashed past me, last resorts if I needed to duck away.

I barreled down the hallway, a rough plan in mind: go back downstairs, return to the caf, and then dive into Mr. Aiden's room. I didn't care if he was alone, or if the room was empty, or if there was a whole class in it. I just had to get there. It was safety.

I made it to the far end of the hall, blasted through the door's meshed glass and hurled myself down the stairs. I rounded a corner and sprinted back to the rear of the caf. My knapsack was lying right where I'd dropped it. Mr. Aiden's class was just around the bend, but before I could get there, two of my pursuers came into view.

Damn!

I tried to reverse my course, head back to the second floor, but an avalanche of footsteps thudding down the stairs told me I'd never make it. I changed direction, turned left, and barreled through the nearest set of cafeteria doors. I stopped quickly, but my heart continued to pound at a full-out pace. Study hall was on and the caf was silent, monitored by a humorless woman who stood at the far end by the stage, scanning the room like a vulture. I slowed to a walk, sweating, out of breath.

There's a rear exit behind the stage, I thought. *If I can get to it, I might be able to get out.*

But even if I did, there was a new problem to face. The exit led to a narrow passage with no side doors. If the Bastards were smart enough to go around and block it off, I'd be trapped like a rat.

I glanced over my shoulder at the doorway I'd just come through. Two guys stopped outside of it. There were two other sets of doors set into the side of the caf. The nearer one was empty, but the Bastards were standing just outside the one further down.

I can cross over, try to make it to that last open door, but there are who-knows-how-many of them and only one of me. And I have further to go. I'll never make it.

The stage exit was the riskiest, but it was the one I had to take. Unfortunately, that meant actually going up on the stage and drawing even more attention to myself. And once that was done, I'd be heading blindly into a narrow passage.

No problem, right?

I walked slowly, carefully, trying to act like I belonged there. I could feel eyes all over me: the predatory glares of the Bastards, the suspicious stare of the monitor, the indifferent looks from the other students. It felt like forever before I reached the stairs that led up to the stage. When I finally arrived, I mounted them one at a time, my heart pounding. I headed into the stage left wing. I put my hand against the exit door and said a silent prayer.

When I opened it, a large, dark figure blocked the passage on the other side. He was facing away from me, but turned in my direction when I opened the door. I immediately recognized the slicked-back hair, the ponytail, the rolled-up sleeves, and the broad shoulders.

The janitor stared at me, amused and curious. "What's the haps?"

I was overwhelmed with relief.

"I'm in deep shit," I said.

A few guys skidded around the corner at the far end of the hallway. When they saw me with the janitor, they turned tail and fled back the way they'd come.[138]

"C'mon," he said, and led me shaking and panting down the hall.

---

[138] It pays to surround yourself with people who are cooler (and tougher) than you.

Chapter Sixteen

I'd never been inside the custodian's room, although I had peeked inside once or twice when I was passing by. School legend had it that the custodians smoked in there, but how could they get away with lighting up inside a school?

He led me down a short entry hall, past rickety shelves crowded with rolls of paper towels and bottles of cleaning solution. We rounded a corner and entered the main room, which was dark and very warm. The walls were lined with old office desks, their surfaces covered with papers and pop cans, all except for one, which was completely, intriguingly, bare. In front of it were stacked three ancient school chairs. Above the desk, an old industrial fan was embedded in the wall; glowing spots of daylight shone between its blades. Without a word, the janitor hoisted two chairs on top of the desk, pulling the third one over as a stepstool. He climbed up, took a seat, and removed a cigarette from a pack he pulled from his pocket.

He held out his hand to help me up. I was still shaken and very thankful for the strength of his fingers as they gripped mine.

He lit his cigarette, holding its glowing ember up to the fan. Although the blades weren't moving, the smoke was still drawn outside.

Mystery solved.

He held the pack out to me. With trembling fingers, I removed a cigarette and he lit it for me.

We sat in the cave-lit gloom for a few moments, staring at our little fires as they glowed in the darkness of the room. The thin lines of smoke rising from our cigarettes bent in mid-air as they were drawn outside.

Without taking the cigarette out of his mouth, the janitor held out his hand. I could see the word ROCK inked[139] across his knuckles. "Derek."

I shook his hand. "Shel."

We returned to our silence, quietly inhaling and exhaling.

Eventually Derek said, "Looks like you got yourself in some trouble."

"Yeah."

"You wanna talk about it?"

"It's just these guys, they're giving me a hard time because ..."

Derek seemed like a cool guy, but I barely knew him. I

---

139 At this time, tattoos were still a novelty, the purview of sailors, carneys, cons, and rock stars. Now everyone has one, even me.

wasn't ready to tell him my whole story. "... because they're bastards."

"You tell the school about it?"

I shook my head.

He said, "Yeah, I know. It's like, 'What's the point?' Right?"

I nodded in agreement. The cigarette was making me feel lightheaded.

"What about your parents? You tell them?"

"Nah."

"Friends?"

I shrugged.

He leaned forward, resting his elbows on his knees. "That's your problem, right there. These guys that are hassling you? These little pricks? They're like those hyenas out in Africa. You know what I'm talking about? They circle around a herd of wildebeests," he moved his finger in a slow loop to demonstrate, "just waiting for one of them to split off from the pack. Maybe it's young, or old, or sick. Whatever. What I'm saying is, when you're alone, you're weak. That's when you get taken down."

He seemed to make sense, but I was still too freaked out to take it all in.

He crushed his cigarette on the edge of the fan, leaving a fresh black streak next to a hundred other marks just like it. He dropped the butt into an empty pop can and lit up a new smoke.

"Look, brother. I don't know what's going on with you; I don't know what kind of shit you got yourself into, but I can see it's tough. So let me give you some advice. These guys, they see you're alone. They know they can get at you. And they'll keep coming at you unless you get more people on your side. You need to tell somebody. I know all this firsthand, man."

It was hard to imagine anyone bullying him, even as a kid.

"You don't believe me?" He looked right in my eyes. "When I was in school, I used to *be* one of those pricks."

He turned his head to peer through the blades of the fan. "I clean up shit every day. That's life as a janitor, man. But when people give me a hard time about it, I just flip 'em off." He held up the middle fingers of both tattooed hands, the fingers flashing a c and an o. "I don't need to take that. Work ain't my life. I just do my job all day and play music all night."

"Sounds cool."

"Brother, nobody can make you feel bad about yourself unless you let 'em."

Easy for you to say.

"I know. It sounds like bs, right?"

I said, "These guys, they're such ..." I couldn't finish.

"They can say the nastiest crap they want to about you," he said, pointing his cigarette in my direction. "But you pick how you're gonna react."

I nodded.

I wasn't done my cigarette, but it was making me nauseous. I dropped it into Derek's pop can ashtray. It hissed as it hit whatever liquid remained inside. Derek handed me two sticks of cinnamon gum.[140]

---

140 Big Red. Can you still get that?

"You can't go to class smelling like an ashtray."

"Thanks." I unwrapped the gum and started chewing.

"You were never in here, right?"

Through a mouthful of gum, I said, "Right."

"'Cause then *I'm* the one who's in deep."

As I got down from the desk, Derek said, "Now you got at least one person watching your back, brother."

It was a start.

Chapter Seventeen
————

My parents were out, so I had the whole place to myself while I worked on my speech. For courage, at least that's what I told myself, I had taken some vodka from the liquor cabinet. I'd planned on just taking a few pulls, then topping up the bottle with water, but before I knew it, I'd downed half.

I was sitting on the edge of my bed, holding my face in my hands. My head was spinning, not just from the alcohol, but also from the thought of what I was planning on doing. I picked up my notebook. By the light of my bedside lamp, I looked at what I'd just written.

How can I read that out loud?

It was impossible. I couldn't do it.

But I had to. People needed to know what was happening

or I'd wind up getting the crap beat out of me, just like Bill had said.

I drew a huge x over everything I'd written, then tore out the page, balled it up, and threw it across my room. Feverishly, I wrote down every angry word, every insult, every piece of frustrated hate I could think of, then tossed the entire notebook to the ground and kicked it across the room. For good measure, I stood up and kicked the bed, too, hard. It felt so good that I kicked it again, even harder this time. The bed skittered away at an angle and struck the wall. I tore away the blanket and threw it to the ground. I launched an attack on my room, scratching away at the wallpaper, tearing open my dresser drawers, ripping down posters, spilling garbage across the floor.

I stood in the middle of the wreckage, breathing heavily.

I wasn't done yet.

I grabbed my pillow and swung it through the air. It hit the wall, bounced off, and struck my bedside lamp, which fell to the ground, sparking and flashing. The lamp went dark and the whole room dropped into shadow.

I wiped angry tears from my eyes.

An acrid odor hit my nostrils. I fumbled through my darkened room until I found the switch for the overhead light. The bare bulb flared above me and in its harsh light I could see the broken lamp laying in the middle of the destroyed remains of my room. The lamp was wrapped in a thin cloud of smoke. I took a step toward it, tripped on the mess covering my floor, and fell on my face. Dizzy from drinking, I crawled over to where it had fallen. I picked up the lamp and sat down on the edge of my bed. The shade had come away, revealing the shattered glass egg of the bulb. The lamp was still plugged in, and it made an ominous buzzing sound. The broken inner workings looked ugly and dangerous, like a poisonous insect.

The thin and jagged edge of the glass reflected a hot white light. I pressed the broken bulb against the fragile skin of my wrist.

It would be so easy, I thought, *so easy ...*

All I had to do was drag the serrated glass across my wrist and it would all be over.

I wouldn't have to take any crap from anyone, and I wouldn't have to do what I was planning on doing.

It seemed so simple, like nothing at all.

I pushed the fractured edge hard into my wrist. The skin began to buckle and redden. I felt a sharp pinch, and a ruby red bead of blood appeared on my wrist. I pushed even harder. Soon, a line of scarlet dots had formed. They merged into a trickle that ran down my arm. It hurt so much more than I thought it would, but I knew I was getting close. I just had to start dragging it back and forth ...

The glass cracked from the force I was putting on it, and the lamp jumped forward, slashing across my hand. I howled in pain, dropping the lamp to the floor.

A long, thin crescent of glass was sticking out of the meatiest part of my palm. I pulled it out and threw it away, then curled up on the chaos of my bed, squeezing my bloody arm to my chest.

I was sitting in class, anxiously awaiting my turn to speak. I looked down at the index cards I was holding, copied quickly and messily from the page I'd torn from my notebook. My head hurt and my hands were shaking so badly that the words were just an inky blur. Dan was sitting beside me, but I didn't look over at him for fear of losing my nerve.

I was wearing a long-sleeved dress shirt over the T-shirt I'd bought at the record store. When it came time to do my speech, my plan was to unbutton the over-shirt, revealing what I wore beneath it.

If I have the courage, that is.

The long sleeves didn't quite hide the dotted line of scabs that ran like Morse code across my left wrist. I pulled the cuff down a little further.

Kelly, who had earlier bragged about her many successes in the area of public speaking, was at the front of the class, delivering an ingratiating and predictably well-prepared speech on the topic of "My Favorite Day of the Week."[141] I tried—unsuccessfully—to calm myself as she spoke of the mythical origins of the names of days ("Did you know that Friday, named after the Norse goddess Freya, is the only day of the week named after a woman? Perhaps it's because only a woman can get everything done by Friday!") And the pros and cons of each ("Now, most people dislike Mondays, but I believe that Monday is the best day ... for picking up on the latest gossip!")

Despite the fact that every word she said made me more and more agitated, I hoped that she'd never stop talking,

---

141 I was paying some attention, though, as you will see.

because when she did, it would be my turn to face the class, and I was terrified of what would happen then.

Kelly finished her speech long before I was ready for her to do so. A polite but lackluster round of applause rose and quickly fell.

Mrs. Piedmont called my name. I took a very deep breath and walked to the front of the class. I turned and looked out at the eyes of my fellow students. When I saw Dan staring back at me, I moved my gaze downward. My legs began to shake and, for a moment, I thought I was going to collapse in a heap right there by the chalkboard.

I put my hand on a button of my dress shirt, preparing to undo it, but I stopped. That was a step too far.

I glanced one more time at my notes and began to speak.

I tried to start by saying "Hi," but my voice instantly cracked and I couldn't say the rest of the line.

A few people laughed.

I can't even make it past the first word. How am I going to do this?

I took another deep breath, swallowed, and kept going.

"Hi," I repeated. "A little while ago, because of something that happened to me, I thought that I was gay."

Someone in the room coughed and I stopped talking, losing my nerve once again. I took a moment, exhaled, and carried on.

"So ... this was scary for me, as you can imagine. Then I realized that I wasn't just gay, I was bisexual, which means being attracted to both girls and guys. It was a secret, but then some other people found out about it. Since then, I've had some people stop being friends with me. I guess some people don't like that I'm bi, or don't like the way it makes them feel. Some think that it's just a phase and I'm actually straight, or else I'm all the way gay and just won't admit it. I've made some gay friends, too. Some gay students[142] don't want to be my friend for the same lame reasons as straight people."

I stopped reading and switched to the next card. I tried to read it out loud but nothing happened. My mouth was paralyzed. Whatever momentum I'd had was now lost and I didn't think I could get it back again. I wanted to walk out the door and never come back.

But I've come this far ...

I exhaled, licked my lips, and began to read the second card, one word at a time.

"I've ... read ... a lot ... about this in the last while. I'm going to clear up a few myths. The first myth is that bisexuals are just sexually confused and not really bi at all, and that eventually they will become straight or gay. That's a myth, although people can change over time. And some people actually do come out as bi before they come out as gay, so it's complicated and confusing. But there are millions of bisexual people all over the world. Some people say that everyone is potentially bisexual.[143]

Someone in the class let out a disbelieving huff. I flicked my eyes out to the class and then back to my notes. "The second myth is that people who are bisexual will have

---

142 To say there was more than one is a bit of an exaggeration, but I guess I was going for effect.

143 People like to throw this line out, but many, many others would disagree.

sex with anyone. That's also not true. If you're straight, ask yourself if you're attracted to everyone of the opposite sex. Bisexual people like people of both sexes, but that doesn't mean we want to get it on with everyone. I'm no different than anyone else that way."

I took one deep breath, then another. I was OK. It was getting easier. I flipped to the next card.

"There are a few reasons why I chose this as my speech topic. The first is that this is on my mind a lot right now. The second reason is that when you are gay or bi, you have to talk about it. If you don't, you will go crazy. The final reason is that there are people in this school who have threatened to hurt me, maybe even ..."

I stopped and squeezed my eyes shut.

"... maybe even kill me, just because of who I am. I don't deserve that.

"If these certain people, and they know who they are, had beaten me up or worse before I told you all the truth, then I would probably be too scared to do what I'm doing right now. They might still do it, but at least you'll know why.

"In conclusion, bisexuality is a real thing; bisexuals are real people; and we should all be treated just like everyone else. Someone else here is probably gay or bi. I hope you are all OK."

I exhaled.

"That's it. That's the end."[144]

When I looked up at the class, twenty-five faces stared

---

144 It may have been crazy. It may have been ill-advised. It was barely even a speech (more like a tirade). But I'm proud of myself for having done it. I doubt I could do anything that brave now.

at me in quiet disbelief. I was expecting a chorus of jeers, maybe even a rotten tomato or two, but all I got was stunned silence. I looked over at Mrs. Piedmont, who seemed to be holding back tears.

I wasn't sure I'd be able to do it, but I had. There was no going back now. And just maybe, my life was going to get a whole lot better.

Chapter Eighteen

C LANG!
The side of my face hit a locker. I grunted in shock, surprise, and pain. Bodies crowded in around me, their hands holding me flat against the wall.[145]

I opened my mouth to speak, to yell, to beg, but something thick and soft was shoved inside it. I gagged on it, unable to fight back. A wad of spit hit the side of my face.

Someone leaned in close to me and said, "Fuck you, faggot."

A moment later, I was torn away from the lockers and dragged a few feet down. A bed sheet was thrown over me and everything went white. Through the thin fabric, I could make out the gray forms of my attackers, their identities hidden. I was too terrified to think, to reason. I

---

145 It couldn't have been more than an hour after I'd done my speech, and 20 minutes since school had ended. News travels fast.

felt myself being pushed through a door. I twisted as I fell, and the crown of my head hit something hard. There was a sound, a sharp crack, followed by a moment of excruciating pain. Then the world dropped away into blackness.

When I came to, I was on the floor, slumped against the wall. My vision was hazy, the lights in the ceiling were white blurs.

It's the blanket … not a blanket … a sheet …

I pulled the sheet away from my face and shoved it aside. In the center of the sheet was a bright red slash, ugly, long, and sickeningly wet. I reached up to my mouth and pulled out the gag. It was a once-white sport sock, its sole turned gray from long use.

Spitting and coughing, I moved to my hands and knees. I stuck my fingers in my mouth and dragged my nails against my tongue. I gagged and heaved but didn't throw up.

A volcanic pain flared at the top of my skull. I groaned, holding my head in both hands. It was brutal, an intolerable agony. And then, like a magician's trick, the pain just disappeared. I felt dizzy, but relieved.

Oh, I thought, *it must not be that bad …*

Bright spots began to flash in front of my eyes and I blacked out.

I opened my eyes but couldn't get them to focus. I shook my head to clear my vision. I looked around, trying to figure out where I was. The walls were beige cinderblock, the floor covered in white tile. There was a row of sinks opposite some toilet stalls. No urinals.

Bastards.

They dropped me in the goddamned girls' bathroom. At least it's empty ...

The wall came out slightly, right where I'd first fallen, creating a shallow corner. There was a small red smear on the edge, a few feet off the ground.

That's where I hit.

I tried to stand up but fell over. I reached up, grabbed on to a tampon dispenser, and used it to pull myself up. As I got to my feet, the floor felt like it was tipping dangerously away from me. My vision dragged in and out of focus.

Something warm and liquid was running down my lower back. I reached around, felt a slick film under my fingertips. I brought my hand back and saw that my fingers were coated in hot, thick blood. I reached up and felt the place on my head where it had struck the wall. It was numb to the touch. My fingertips sunk into a deep and wet indentation in my scalp. I began to see lights again.

You took all of those lifeguarding courses.

You know what's going on.

You're in shock, idiot.

I mumbled, "Drink fluids and stay warm ..." then passed out once again.

When I regained consciousness, I crawled to the nearest sink and pulled myself shakily to my feet. I needed to get cleaned up.

But not in here.

Not in the girls' washroom.

The Bastards don't get that.

The sheet lay where it had fallen, pure white except for that hideous badge of red. I gathered it up and shoved it in the garbage.

I opened the door a sliver and peeked out. The Bastards were gone and my knapsack lay on the floor where it had fallen. I picked it up and slipped into the boys' bathroom next door. What I saw in the mirror was frightening. My skin was gray. My hair was dark and matted with blood. I wiped my bloody hand on my shirt, leaving a rusty stain.

Idiot. You can't walk around with bloody clothes.

I took off my dress shirt, revealing the new tee beneath it, black with the letters AC/DC screened across the chest in white.

You can't walk around in that, either.

I balled up the dress shirt and pushed it into the trash. I tried to pull off my tee but all the strength seemed to have left my arms; the muscles seized up like rusting machinery. I tried again. Slowly, and with great effort, I managed to get the shirt off. I turned it inside out and put it back on. Thankfully, the blood would be hard to see against the dark fabric. The logo was still slightly visible as a change in texture. I noticed that while the letters would be backwards to anyone who could make them out, they ran forward when I looked at them in the mirror. It seemed strangely funny.

Ha ha ha ...

I winced as needlelike sparks of pain began to flash

across the wound on my scalp.

I turned on the tap and drank a mouthful of metallic water. Then I dunked my head under the stream, rinsing off my hair. I did my best to dry off with a handful of paper towels.

Soon my head was clearer, but the pain was building again. I went back out into the hall. There was a spattered line of blood droplets running to the girls' bathroom. I didn't have to open the door to know that it looked worse inside.

But I can't go back in and clean it up.

I made my way to the office and told a secretary I'd slipped. She sent me next door to the sick room, where I wrapped myself in a blanket and went right to sleep.[146]

"Son?"

A deep voice dragged me out of my pain-addled daze.

"Wake up, son. We're sending you to Outpatients, to the hospital."

I looked up into the eyes of my vice-principal, who was staring at me through thick glasses. He was sitting on the edge of the cot, dressed in a gray suit and tie. Thankfully, I'd had no dealings with him in all my time at school. He was a notorious hard-ass.

"Are you OK?" he asked.

"Yeah."

"Tell me what happened," he said.

"I fell down."

"Like hell, son. You were pushed down."

---

146 Probably not a good sign.

"No," I said quietly.

"There's a hell of a lot of blood in the girl's washroom by the gym, and a trail of it leading here. That's not yours?"

"No."

"I want to help you."

"I'm fine."

He raised himself up slightly, then sat down again, resting his elbows on his knees and linking his fingers.

"Bull," he said firmly. "Something's happened, and I need to know what's going on in my school."

You've got no clue what goes on in your school.

"Nothing. I just fell down. I'm OK now."

"I need to know what's going on in my school!" he barked. A fine spray of saliva hit my face.

"Nothing!" I snapped back.

He reached down, below my line of sight, and lifted up the bloody sheet and dress shirt. I felt sick and closed my eyes.

"So you don't know anything about this?"

"No," I said.

"Never seen it before?"

"No."

I heard him drop the bloody fabric and reopened my eyes.

He leaned back, seeming to realize that he was getting nothing more out of me.

"You've bled all over the pillow," he said. "We're calling you a cab to take you to the hospital. We'll call your parents and tell them where you are."

I wanted to demand that he *not* tell my parents, but one look into his stony face and I knew it was hopeless. I sat up stiffly and shambled to the front doors with the vice-principal as my silent escort. He waited with me, unspeaking, until the cab came. When it did, he handed me a taxi chit[147] and walked away.

I sat down in the front seat beside the cabbie.

"Where to?" he asked.

"Outpatients," I said.

"Outpatients? Is that the same as Emerg?"[148]

"I don't know. It's where I was told to go."

He pulled down his handheld radio and said into it, "Central, is Outpatients the same as Emerg?" A fuzzy voice replied that it was. He hung the radio back up and headed down the driveway.

"What's going on?" he asked.

"I hit my head," I replied.

He looked at the crusty mass of my hair. "Are you bleeding?"

"Yeah."

"Then don't lean against the seat, man!"

I tried to lean forward but my seatbelt held me in place.

He reached over and clicked off the belt.

The pain was building again and my head began to swim.

He said, "Damn, man. They should have put a bandage on you or something."

I sat in the waiting room, sprawled in a plastic chair, phasing in and out of consciousness. Old sitcoms buzzed

---

147 A little slip of paper that tells the taxi to charge the school for the ride.
148 Emerg = the Emergency department.

from the TV overhead. I sat through *Three's Company*, *Soap*, and *Barney Miller*[149] until I was eventually called in and told to change into a hospital gown. I waited for a while in a frigid, curtained-off exam room until a white-haired doctor arrived.

He looked at my wound. "So, what the hell happened to you?"

"I fell against a wall."

"Fell against a wall, huh?" He pulled on some gloves and peered at my bloody crown. "Looks a little sharp for a wall."

"It was the corner of a wall."

"Is that so?" he said, sounding unconvinced. "OK, follow my finger." He held up his index finger, moved it left, right, up, and down. I followed it with my eyes. "Any dizziness? Fainting?"

"Only when it first happened."

He asked, "What day is it today?"

"Wednesday."

"You'll be fine," he said, peeling off his gloves. "We'll clean up the wound and put a few stitches in it."

He tossed the gloves in the trash and left the room.

I lay back down. Without really knowing why, I thought of Jenny, of all the crap we'd been through. How she'd looked and sounded so different that time I'd seen her writing in her book behind the school. I thought of how, a hundred years ago, I'd spent a warm spring night kissing her in the front seat of the car.

---

149 I'm sure you could find them on YouTube; just don't expect Shakespeare.

A tall nurse came in carrying some supplies and set them on a metal tray. She told me to roll over. I held onto the loose edge of my gown and turned over onto my stomach. She told me to lift my head, and placed a folded towel under my face. From the corner of my eye I could see a rusty patch of blood on the pillow where I'd been lying.

"Some cold water," she said matter-of-factly. An icy stream poured over my wound. It ran over the back of my head and then down my face, soaking the towel. I felt her dab at my injured scalp. It hurt like hell. "Just hold that position while I prep the area." I felt something pulling on my scalp, then heard the *shink-shink* sound of scissors cutting hair.

"How much are you taking off?" I asked, frightened of looking even worse the next day.

"Just a little bit around the cut. You won't even notice it."

Sure, I won't ...

I tried to crane my neck so I could see her better.

"Don't move," the nurse said sternly. I felt a razor nip sharply at my skin as she shaved the area.

"Ow."

"Just about finished," she said, making a few more swipes with the razor. "All done, Tiger. The doctor will be back in a few minutes. Just keep that position." She gathered her equipment and left. My wound, now open to the air, felt both hot and cold at the same time.

Another nurse parted the curtain and asked, "Sheldon?"

"Yeah?"

"I talked to your father. He wants to know if you need him to pick you up."

I didn't relish the thought of walking all the way home, but the thought of trying to explain to my father what had happened was even worse.

"No, I can find my own way back."

"You sure?"

"Yeah."

She left. I considered putting my clothes back on and walking right out of the building, but then the doctor came back in.

"All ready?" he asked.

"I guess," I said.

He pulled up a chair and swiveled a metal armature. Peeking sideways, I could see him pick up a small curve of metal.

"Face down," he ordered. I turned so that my nose was pushed into the firm cushioning of the hospital bed.

"This will desensitize the area," he said. I felt a sharp stabbing pain at the site of my wound.

"Ow."

"Easy, there," he said. "All done." The pain began to lessen almost immediately, replaced by a thick throbbing sensation.

He started stitching. I could feel the needle pushing and pulling through the skin around the area.

"So, fell into a wall," he said casually as he worked.

"Yep."

"Were you at school?"

"Yeah."

"Everything OK at school?"

No.

"Yeah."

"At home?"

Fine.

"Fine."

"I see you have some abrasions on your wrist, there. How'd you get those?"

I scrabbled mentally for some plausible explanation. "Caught it on some barbed wire," I said, hoping to sound casual enough to be convincing.

"Was the wire rusty?" he asked.

"No," I replied.

I felt one last pull on my scalp and he said, "OK, all sewed up. Be careful with it for the next few days. Come back in a week or two to have them out."

"Thanks," I replied, pushing myself up to a sitting position.

Somewhat awkwardly, as if he was afraid of embarrassing either of us, the doctor pulled a small business card from his coat pocket and handed it to me. I looked at the card; it was for a crisis hotline.[150]

He cleared his throat. "Just in case," he said.

I nodded.

He gave me a brief smile, parted the curtains, and left.

With aching muscles, I slid off the bed and picked up my clothes, slipping the card into my pants' pocket. The inside-out T-shirt had gone stiff from the dried blood, but there was nothing I could do about that. The tag at the back of the shirt was sticking out, so I picked up a pair of small, bent-

---

150 I'm sure he was doing his best here, but I'd like to think that if this happened today, such an obvious case would be followed up more thoroughly.

arm scissors from the doctor's tray and trimmed it off. Then I pulled the rest of my clothes back on.

I had just dragged myself out into the late-afternoon sunlight, gearing up for the thirty-minute trek home, when I had the sudden and sickening realization that I'd left my knapsack back in the sick room at school. Not only did it hold the remains of my lunch, as well as all my homework, but it also had my notebook, with all its angry, violent venting.

Crap.

I began the half-hour trek back to school.

Chapter Nineteen

By the time I made it to back to school, even the school sports teams were finishing for the day. I let myself into the sick room and found the knapsack tucked under the cot, right where I'd left it. I took the Appendix exit and trudged around the outside of the school, hoping to avoid any encounters.

The teachers' parking lot[151] was still half-full. Exhausted football players were lugging their gear down from the elevated sports field. A car tore across my path, spewing a cloud of dust into the air, making me cough.

That's right, world, spit all your crap on me.

I obviously deserve it.

Bring it on.[152]

---

151 For anyone who says that teachers make too much money for what they do, I encourage you to check out the collection of Honda Civics in your average teachers' parking lot.

152 This attitude, while easy to adopt when times are tough, is not attractive or

I was headed across the parking lot when I saw a tall figure in running gear[153] coming down the embankment. It was Mr. Aiden.

I wasn't sure if I was relieved to see a friendly face after all that had happened, or afraid that he'd ask me why I looked so rough. He went over to his car, a small blue hatchback, and opened the back.

He saw me, waved, and I walked the short distance to where he stood.

"Hi, Sheldon. Staying late?" he asked. He pulled a gray sweatshirt from the car and used it to wipe the sweat from his face, arms, and neck.

"Yeah," I mumbled.

"Everything all right?" he asked.

I shrugged.

"You want a ride home?"

It wasn't far, but the idea of not having to walk another step was very appealing. I nodded. He opened my door for me, closing it once I was in. He went around to the driver's side, opened the door with a confident jerk, and slipped in. He pulled his aviator sunglasses from the dash.

"Where to?" he asked. I said nothing.

I looked at his face and some part of me cracked. I collapsed, falling over onto his shoulder, sobbing, saddened, inflamed. I could smell the salty mix of his cologne and skin. The back of my hand fell against his bare leg.

---

productive. Just a heads up.

153 This is 1980's running gear, not the slick stuff of today. Think Adidas shorts, pastel tank top, and long, stripey white sports socks.

"Sheldon, I can see this is a hard time for you, but I need you to get out of the car."

I couldn't even talk, let alone respond.

"I need you to get out. We can talk more then."

When I spoke, my voice was choked. "Why?" I asked, but I knew the reason. I was acting crazy.

When I refused to leave, Mr. Aiden got out of the car and came around to my side. He opened the passenger door and crouched down beside me.

"It's my fault. I shouldn't have offered you a ride in the first place. But I want to help."[154]

I pushed awkwardly past him and stormed away.

Behind me, I heard him say, "I can walk you home if you like."

Screw you.

I didn't look back.

I was curled up in my bed, drifting in and out of sleep, when I felt someone sit down beside me. I heard my brother say, "Shel. Wake up."

I opened my bleary eyes, squinting against the light and the pain radiating from the top of my head.

Bill put his hand on my shoulder. "I got your message. Why are you asleep? It's only 8:00."

I tried to lift my head, but the stitches were killing me. I reached up and gently touched the site of the wound. I gasped at how much it hurt.

---

154 Before you judge him too harshly, consider the fact that if some rumor got started about him, he could have lost his job. I should also add that it wasn't that unusual for a teacher to give a student a ride back in those days.

Bill leaned over and examined the damage. "Ouch, that's nasty."

"I know. I can feel it."

"It's kind of cool, actually. The way your head's been shaved and stitched up makes it look like a baseball."

"Wonderful. Is it noticeable?"

"Well ..." He checked the area again. "You can probably comb your hair over it. Wear a ball cap when you can."

I said up, wincing.

"Did you take anything for it?"

I rubbed my eyes. "Couple Tylenol."

"What happened?"

I couldn't put it into words.

"Did someone do this to you?"

I nodded.

"Was it because of ... you know ..."

I nodded again.

"How did they find out?"

I opened my eyes and started talking. I talked and talked and didn't stop until I'd told him everything

"Jesus Christ, Shel. This is *exactly* what I told you not to do. And *exactly* what I told you would happen."

"I know. I deserve it, I guess."

"No, you don't. But you could have stopped it from ever happening."

"It's like you said. Every version of my future sucks."

I fell against his shoulder and he put his arm around me.

"That was a shitty thing for me to say. It's not true."

I didn't believe him.

A panicked thought raced into my head. "You didn't tell mom and dad, did you?"

"No, relax. I just made up some BS excuse for being here. Said I had to come get something."

I relaxed a little.

Bill said, "So Mom and Dad don't know? About anything?"

"NO," I said, and from my tone I hoped he knew how much I wanted to keep it that way. "They were at work when it happened."

"I won't tell them but you can't have it both ways. You can't keep it a secret from them and then go tell the whole school. They're bound to find out eventually."

I knew he was right. But I hoped and hoped that I could keep it a secret for just a little bit longer.

"I need more time," I said.

"I know, but you can't go on like this. You've got to do something."

I pleaded with him. "Don't tell Mom and Dad. I'm BEGGING you, seriously."

"I won't. But you've got to do something."

"What?"

"I don't know. Something."

Chapter Twenty

The next day, I wore an old baseball hat whenever I could, trying to hide my bald spot and stitches. My nerves were so bad that I felt like I could lose it at any time. I was so worried about getting caught by the Bastards that I plotted out all my routes far in advance, ensuring that they would never catch me unawares. I slipped out of my second-period class fifteen minutes early so I could make it to Mr. Aiden's while everyone else was still locked down.

Mr. Aiden.

He was all wrapped up in my thoughts, too. When I'd finally calmed down the night before, I started feeling bad for taking off on him like I had. He was trying to help, after all. I hoped to have the chance to apologize, although I was pretty sure he'd act like nothing had happened.

I arrived at his room with plenty of time to spare, but my

feeling of success was cut short when I saw that Andrew was the only one inside the darkened room. I'd never really gotten over how he made me feel on the day we first met.

He sat with his feet up on a desk, arms crossed, quietly fuming. His face was a mask of silent rage. I had seen him in some bad moods but not like this. I had no idea what had happened to him.[155] I stopped short, hoping that he hadn't seen me, but it was no good. I'd been spotted.

"Are you in or out?" he asked with a furious smirk.

I stood paralyzed in the doorway. Was there a right answer to his question?

"In, I guess."

He said, "Of course you are," as if he knew some big secret. He went back to glaring out the window.

I selected a desk close enough to the door for a quick escape, but not so far from Andrew that it looked like I was shying away from him. I plunked down in a chair and reached inside my bag for my lunch. If no one else showed up, I'd eat a small portion of it, feign a need to be somewhere else, then bail out as soon as possible. Andrew may have been on my team, but he sure as hell wasn't a team player. I didn't want to spend another second alone with him, not in his current state, anyway.

Without even looking up, he said, "Nice hat."

Reflexively, I looked up to the brim of my ball cap.

"Thanks," I replied dully.

"HA!" His laughter was a short, derisive burst. What he found so amusing escaped me.

---

155 And I never found out, either. These things just came and went.

He went back to ignoring me and we sat together in a pained silence.

I asked, "Do you know where everyone is?"

"Darren's at some meeting or other. I don't know about the rest of the homos."

That was it. I'd had it with his casual insults.

"Why do you do that?" I asked, demanding an answer.

"Do what?" he replied, turning toward me with fire in his eyes.

"Put people down all the time."

"I'm just having a laugh. It's not my fault that no one else gets the joke."

"Mr. Aiden's trying to help you, right? Help all of us. So why are you so hard on him?"

"Darren Aiden is pathetic. We're the best part of his sad, sad life."

"What the hell do you know about him?"

"I know all about *your* favorite teacher."

"What are you talking about?"

"Don't act so stupid. You've got the hots for him so bad. You'd have to be blind not to see it."

Was I really so obvious?[156]

My anger finally got the best of me.[157] "What the hell did I ever do to you to make you hate me so much?"

"Sorry to disappoint you, but you don't mean jack to me, Switch." He spit out the last word like it was poison. I could feel it sizzling in my blood.

"Because I'm bi? That's your problem?"

---

156 Probably.
157 Which, I see now, is probably what Andrew wanted all along.

"You don't get it and you never will!"

"Why don't you tell me what 'IT' is?"

"You ..." he stopped short, fuming. For the first time ever, I saw the ever-cool Andrew at a loss for words. "You have a home to go to at night?"

"Of course, what difference ..."

He cut me off before I could finish my question. "Do you have parents that will love you no matter what?"

"Yeah." I hoped so, anyway.

"Then you have NOTHING to complain about. You mope around ..." He made a clownish, exaggerated face of misery. "... acting like you're the only person that the world has ever taken a shit on. You don't know anything!"

"I don't think I'm the only person who's got it bad!"

"Timmy-Boy ..." He gestured to the rear of the room where Tim usually sat. "His father put him in the hospital when he caught him fooling around with some kid. And my folks kicked me out on the street. So the next time you go whining about how rough you've got it, you can shove it up your ass."

I ripped my hat off and leaned over to show him the scars. "Take a look at that and tell me I don't have it rough!"

He looked at the wound for a moment. In a quiet voice he said, "Maybe your wife can look after it for you." He kicked the edge of his desk so it spun 45 degrees, facing directly away from me. He picked up a magazine and sat down heavily, spreading the pages with a flourish.

I don't have to take that!

I should take one of these chairs and bust it over his stylish head!!!

But I didn't. I shouldered my backpack and marched out of the room.

Chapter Twenty-One

I knew I was skipping class and I knew I'd get caught, but I couldn't face school, not with Andrew and the vice-principal and the Bastards and everyone else. I ploughed through the back doors and began stumping my way home.

In my head, I cursed them all. I cursed them individually, in small groups, and as one large and detestable mass. I cursed them and cursed them until my breathing finally slowed, my heart stopped racing, and my mouth had gone dry. I'm sure I was still mumbling curses when I passed by Duncan's house.

I heard his low, slow voice call out to me, "Hey."

I stopped in the middle of the sidewalk and turned around.

Wonderful, I thought, *one more thing to deal with.*

He was standing in his driveway, wearing jean cut-offs and a gray Adidas T-shirt, holding a basketball under one arm.

"You done school?" he asked.

"Yeah."

"You wanna shoot hoops?"

I was stunned. Here I was, feeling like the whole world hated me, and now Duncan, of all people, was asking me to hang out with him. We'd barely said two words to each other our whole lives.

What am I going to do otherwise?

Sit at home by myself and watch soap operas for the rest of the day?

"Sure. Why the hell not?"

There was a battered old basketball court near The Woods, which meant we didn't have to go very far.

"Cool," he replied. He was unreadable, his face pasty and indifferent. I had no clue what he was thinking.

I said, "I need to drop my stuff at home and get something to drink."

"Just leave it here," he said and led me through his front door. The layout of the house wasn't too different from mine, but the inside was a mess, decorated in unpleasant shades of rust and brown.

He pointed to a heap of old newspapers and flyers. "Set your stuff over there."

I set my bag down and he disappeared out of sight. My heart rate began to pick up again.

I've seen this kind of set-up before, I thought. *It's in a million horror movies. One minute you're invited into a stranger's house, the next you're chained up in the basement while some psycho cuts you up with an electric carving knife ...*

My paranoid fantasies were broken by the distant sound of two cans opening, followed by the unmistakable noise of someone rummaging around in an overcrowded cabinet. Finally, Duncan returned with two opened cans wrapped in foam holders. Only the silver tops of the cans were visible. He also had a gym bag that I guessed was full of refills.

"Cheers," he said, handing me one and tipping his up. I took a swig and I almost choked. I was expecting cola or something but it was beer. I did my best to act cool, taking a long pull from my can.

Drinking beer in the middle of the day?

Doesn't this guy ever go to school?

"Cheers," I said when I was done.

"Let's go," he said in that slow, distant voice of his, and headed for the door, can in hand.

A flood of questions flowed into my brain.

Is he serious?

Walking down the street with beers in our hands?

At noon?

On a Thursday?

In eyeshot of the school we're cutting?

I followed him out onto the oil-strained driveway. "You, uh, do this a lot?"

"Do what?" he asked.

"You know, cut class, drink beer in the middle of the day?"

"I'm part-time," he said, as if that explained everything.

We walked along the road, taking the occasional sip from our beers. Duncan loped beside me like a teenaged caveman. Every once in a while, he'd take the basketball out from under his arm and dribble it a bit. Surprisingly, I started feeling better, freer than I had in days. Maybe it was because we were being so brazen. Maybe it was the beer.[158]

As we neared our destination, I started feeling downright happy. When I closed my eyes and turned to face the sky, I felt the sun warming my slightly tipsy[159] head. We rounded the curve of The Woods and arrived at the court. It was more dilapidated than I remembered. The pavement was cracked, the netting gone, the hoop bent, but it didn't bother me.

Duncan set the basketball down and pulled off his shirt. For someone who was shaggy from the eyebrows on up, he was remarkably pale and hairless from the neck down. His slightly flabby skin glistened with sweat. He was strong, though, stronger than me.

I turned my baseball hat around backwards and we started playing a little one-on-one. He was big enough to muscle me out of the way when he needed to, but he was also slow and lacked any kind of finesse. Even my half-assed court skills would have beaten him if I'd cared enough to play hard. Mostly we just screwed around, taking turns at the net, goofing around with fadeaways and hook

---

158 I can't really justify any of my actions here. If you get caught drinking and cutting class, remember: You didn't get the idea from me.
159 On half a beer. I was always a lightweight.

shots. After fifteen minutes or so, we cracked open our second beers. Without saying a word, we began a race to see who could finish theirs the fastest. Duncan won easily. To celebrate his victory, he tossed his empty can over his shoulder and into the grass.

Although we had now spent some time together, I didn't know Duncan any better than I ever had. I kept wondering what was going on in his head.

Is he that much of an outcast that he wants me for a friend?
Is he a man of mystery or just a lunkhead?

"Let's go back," he said. He picked up his shirt, wiped his face down with it, and then bunched it up under his arm.

"ok," I replied, happy to go with the flow.

Duncan led the way. He led us through a sparse patch of field grass and into the Woods. It wasn't a shortcut by any means, but going through the Woods was an acceptable route home for anyone heading our way. I did it all the time.

All draped in the bright green leaves of spring, the Woods looked fairly picturesque, as long as you didn't look down at all the garbage. Halfway in, we approached a large, rectangular block of stone that was known, not too creatively, as the Rock. It had long served as a bench, meeting place, and unofficial center of the Woods. It kind of looked like an altar, and the beer cans, stray clothes, and condom wrappers lying around it were like sacrifices we all made to the god of bad behavior.

Duncan said, "Hold here for a sec," and threw his t-shirt down on the Rock. I sat down beside his shirt and waited while he went a few steps into the woods. He stopped and began to relieve himself. He was so close, I could hear the wet spatter. It made me feel uneasy, but I couldn't say exactly why.

When he was done, he turned around and crossed the few steps back toward me. I was about to stand when he said, "Don't get up."

He sat down beside me, not speaking, not even moving, just staring blankly into the woods. I turned toward him, wondering what was going on. He put his arm, warm and heavy, around my shoulders, like an adult about to offer some worldly advice. It seemed like such a strange thing for him to do. He ran his arm down my spine, then up and under my shirt, caressing my back. His hand felt huge and strong.

"You wanna?" he asked.

I knew then why he'd asked me here, why he'd been so friendly. My stomach felt like it was wheeling around inside of me. I froze, completely uncertain of what to do or what to say. Sure, I wanted to be with a guy the way I'd been with Jen. But with Duncan? I barely knew him. And in the Woods, of all places?

I looked around at the thin light spilling through the scraggly trees, at the muddy paths that traced through the forest, and at the garbage-strewn ground. There was no one there but us, and still plenty of time before school let out. We'd hear anyone coming a mile away.

I couldn't believe what was happening. My entire body thrummed with a mixture of pleasure and unease.

I looked into his eyes and, for the first time ever, I saw Duncan smile. He pulled off my baseball cap and ran his fingers through my messy hair. He touched my stitches and I cringed.

He asked, "What happened to your head?"

"Nothing," I replied.

"Does it hurt?"

"Yeah."

He pulled my head to his shoulder, and touched his lips to the spot where I'd been hurt.

Then he leaned forward, kissing me softly on the lips. I decided to say yes.

A short time later, we were leaving the Woods, blinking in the bright light and finishing our third beers as we headed home. In our brief time together on the Rock, I'd gone further with a guy than I ever had before.[160]

We walked in silence. Duncan had once again become as unreadable as a sphinx.

The whole thing felt bizarre. Just minutes before, we had been together in the shade of the Woods, and now here we were, out under the glare of the unblinking sun, as if we were fooling it into thinking nothing had happened. I felt dizzy. My fingers tingled and my head spun. I stared at the ground as we walked, trying to hold myself together.

A few moments later, Duncan raised his hand. I looked up and saw some guys crossing the far side of the field. They

---

160 Admittedly, I was starting at basically zero, so going further didn't require much. Let's say, second or third base, depending on your definition.

shot him back a wave. I wondered what they thought of us, walking together.

Can they tell what we've done?

I needed to make sense of what had happened between us. I wanted to talk about it. I *needed* to talk about it. And although I could tell that Duncan had no interest in talking about it, I couldn't stop myself.

I opened my mouth to speak, but Duncan interrupted me before I could even begin.

"I don't want to talk about it," he said.

"But, we just ..."

"I said, I don't want to talk about it."

"Why not?"

"That's how you get in trouble." He gave me a hard, knowing stare.

Guess he's not as clueless as he looks.

He turned his eyes back to the path in front of us. "Don't tell anyone."

"Yeah. For sure."

Wasn't it obvious that I'd keep my mouth shut?[161]

When we got to his place, I grabbed my stuff and thanked him for the beer.

"No problem," he said. "My Dad'll never notice."

I had a million questions to ask him. How long had he known about himself? Who else had he been with? Did he want to be with me again?

We made eye contact and I could tell that he wanted to say something, to reach out to me in some way but, instead,

---

161 Actually, based on my past behavior, no.

he just said, "See ya around," and closed the door, leaving me alone on his doorstep.

Part Three

Chapter Twenty-Two

A few days had passed since the attack and things were returning to normal, whatever that was. I had been thinking about Duncan a lot, even though I hadn't seen him since the day I'd skipped school. The only class I'd actually missed on that day was English, and I never even got in trouble for it. Mrs. Piedmont must have cut me a break.

I was spacing out in her class when the general hubbub around me went silent. I looked around the room. Everyone was staring at me.

"And so, Mr. Bates will be representing this class at the finals, perhaps even representing the school at the regionals."

Me? I won the speech competition?

"Congratulations," she said to me, "and good luck." Facing the entire class, she added, "We're also looking for ballot counters, so if any of you are interested in volunteering, let me know."

An arm shot straight up beside me, silent, straining, and furious. It was Kelly, who had done her speech on the days of the week. Her face was flushed red. Tears were welling in her eyes. With obvious reluctance, Mrs. Piedmont nodded in her direction.

Kelly's voice was choked as she said, "That's totally not fair!"

"And why is that?"

"Well ... he ... he didn't ... he read right from cue cards."

Mrs. Piedmont considered this for a moment. "That may be true, but oration is as much art as science. And the basic elements were there."

"But ..." Kelly struggled for words. "I *know* people voted my speech higher."

Cutting a surprisingly formidable figure, Mrs. Piedmont stared her down. "Don't forget," she snapped, "that I have a say in the selection as well. And it *was* a very effective speech."

Kelly folded her arms, fuming.

"Does that answer your question?" Mrs. Piedmont asked.

"May I be excused?" Kelly asked, but before our teacher could respond, she had stormed out of the room.

I peeked my head into Room 115. "Mr. Aiden?" I had a lot I wanted to talk to him about.

"Oh, hi, Sheldon."

"Is it too early to come in?"

"No, not at all."

Relieved, I entered the room and set my knapsack down at a desk close to the front. I saw Tim at the back, occupied with a pen and paper rather that his usual computer. I waved but he didn't see me.

I can't say I was sad that Andrew wasn't there; I'd been walking on eggshells around him ever since our big blow-out. When I saw him the day after, I thought he was going to get right back into it with me. Instead, he acted as if nothing had happened. I decided to do the same and had kept my distance ever since.

Nervously, I asked Mr. Aiden, "Can I talk to you for a minute?" I felt like I was violating an unwritten rule of the room by being so direct. After all, Mr. Aiden didn't become involved in our lives, he just gave us space to be, which was more than most of us had otherwise. But these were special circumstances.

He seemed a little taken aback, but his dark eyes were inquisitive.

"Sure, what can I help you with?"

"Well, first, I'm sorry I freaked out on you the other day."

With practiced calm, he said, "Not a problem. Are you feeling better?"

"Yeah. But now I've got something else going on."

"What's up?"

"Well, I wrote this speech for Mrs. Piedmont's class ..."

"I heard."

"How?"

"Oh, you know. People talk."

Yeah, I did know. And the teachers probably gossiped just as much as the students.

"I guess," I said. "So, yeah. I wrote this speech. I was really upset when I wrote it, but I felt like, like I needed to do it. It was really ..." the right words escaped me, "... honest, I guess."

"It must have been a very hard thing to do."

That's an understatement.

"Yeah. The thing is, I won the contest."

His eyes widened behind his gold-framed glasses. "Really?" he said, with genuine surprise.

"Really. And now I have to do it in front of the whole school."

"What do you know? Is this something you feel you can do?" he asked.

"I don't know. Part of me wants to, but I think it's only going to make my life worse. Know what I mean?"

"I think so."

"So what should I do?" I asked.

He leaned back in his chair. "Well," he said, "I don't know. I can't tell you what to do. That's really something you've got to decide for yourself."

Can't I get a little more help than that?

"But, I don't know ... I mean ..."

"What I *can* say, Sheldon, is that no matter what choice you make, it will be the right one for you."

"I guess." I didn't know what else to say. I suppose I was

hoping for some kind of perfect miracle of an answer.

"I hear some people have been harassing you. Is that still happening?"

It had been days since anyone had given me a hard time. Not only had they stopped bugging me, I hadn't even seen them around. Not since the attack.

"Not really," I said.

He smiled warmly and I thought I saw something in his eye, something ... knowing. "I thought that might happen."

I wondered then just how much the other teachers knew, and what sorts of things were going on behind the scenes, things I'd probably never know.

Then Mr. Aiden leaned in close to me and lowered his voice. "Now, I'm wondering if you can do something for me."

I tried not to let my imagination get the best of me.

"I'm wondering if you can check in with Tim. Just, you know, see how he's doing. OK?"

I felt like I had enough to do just looking after myself but said, "Sure."

I walked reluctantly to the back of the room where Tim was bent over a notebook.

"Hey, Tim." I said.

His head popped up and his eyes bugged out behind their thick glasses, making him look even odder than usual. He composed himself enough to say, "Hi."

"Uh ... mind if I sit back here with you?"

"OK."

It was hard to tell whether he wanted me there or not,

but I sat down and pulled out my lunch. "How's everything going?"

"Fine." He looked a little panicky, like a scared rat.

Definitely not fine, I thought.

Seeing his notebook, I asked, "What are you working on? Homework?"

"No. Stuff I've got to do. I'm getting organized."

It was just vague enough to make me worried. I knew what could happen if you were pushed far enough. From what I knew of Tim, which wasn't much, he'd been pushed pretty far. I was concerned, but didn't want to say anything to scare him off.

"Getting organized is good." I looked back over my shoulder to see if Mr. Aiden was keeping an eye on us. He wasn't.[162]

We passed a moment of awkward silence, and I began to wonder if I should just leave. Tim leaned in and whispered, "Can you keep a secret? For real?"

"Sure, I guess."

"No, *for real*, can you keep a secret?" Everything about him became suddenly intense. It was almost scary.

"Yeah," I said, "I can keep a secret."

"I'm leaving my aunt's house. I can't stand it anymore."

"Whoa. That's really serious. What's going on?"

"I hate her. She's driving me crazy. She's my dad's sister. She's almost as bad as him."

"My parents drive me crazy, too," I said.

---

162 I'm sure he was.

He looked at me like I was comparing a hand grenade to Hiroshima.

"Anyway, just so you know, I won't be around. Don't tell anyone until I've left."

"Where are you going to stay?"

"I'm still figuring it out."

"Is there anything I can do?"

"No."

"You can call me if you need anything."

"Sure."

"Let me give you my phone number." I reached over to take his pen, but he grabbed his notebook and held it to his chest.

"That's private," he said.

I scribbled my phone number on a scrap of paper.

"There," I said, handing it to him. He snatched it away and stuffed it in his pocket.

I asked him, "You're OK, right?"

He stared at me with an indecipherable expression.

I went back to my desk and ate the rest of my lunch in silence.

Chapter Twenty-Three

When English class ended and everyone was leaving, Mrs. Piedmont said, "Sheldon, can you stay behind for a moment?"

Instead of leaving class with everyone else, I pushed against the current of people until I made it to her desk.

"Are you excited about doing your speech for the school?"

If by excited you mean uncertain, nauseous, terrified ...

"Sure."

"Wonderful! I wanted to let you know that you're allowed make minor changes based on any feedback you received."

The only feedback I'd had so far consisted of Kelly's little fit and getting my head cracked open. Dan had heard my speech, but he hadn't said anything to me in days.

"Oh. OK."

"There was one more thing I wanted to tell you but it's

completely slipped my mind ... Oh, well, it will come to me later, I'm sure."

"Thanks." I turned to walk away.

"Oh! I've just thought of it." With an air of mock chastisement, she said, "You still haven't returned your class copy of *Tess of the d'Urbervilles*."

"I'll look for it," I replied.

I hadn't opened my locker in weeks. The book was probably in there along with who knows what else.

That night, I'd just finished making macaroni and cheese[163] and was standing around eating a bowl of it when the phone rang. Being in the kitchen, and with my hands full, it took me a few second to get to the phone, but I managed to pick it up on the sixth ring.[164]

"Hello?" I said.

"Hi."

The voice on the other end was very quiet, and a little uneven, but clearly feminine.

"Jen?"

"Yeah. Hi, Shel." I pressed the phone hard against my ear, as if doing so would bring us that much closer to each other.

"Wow ... what's going on?" I asked, barely concealing my excitement at hearing her voice.

"Not much."

"It's been a while," I said.

"Yeah, sorry. I've been busy."

---

163 From a box, the high point of my culinary skill at the time.
164 We had no voicemail in those days; it just rang and rang until the caller gave up.

"Me, too."

From the warble in her voice, I could tell she was shaken. "I have something to talk to you about."

I tried to switch hands so I could set my bowl down but the fork fell out and hit my foot. "Ow! Crap."

"What?"

"I just dropped macaroni and cheese on my sock."

She laughed. "Dork. You gonna live?"

"Yeah, I think I'll survive. Hold on a sec." I set the phone down while I picked up the fork and the stray macaroni. I picked up the receiver once more. "OK, I'm back."

"I have something I have to tell you, or I guess ask you."

"All right," I said. There was no response, just silence on the other end. I asked, "You still there?"

"Yeah, I'm still here. It's just hard to talk about."

A million terrible scenarios flashed through my head.

She's pregnant.

She's sick.

She's really sick.

She's dying.[165]

"It's OK, Jen, just tell me."

"Well, there's another stupid rumor going around. I wanted you to know what people were saying. And I wanted you to know that I don't believe it, all right?"

"If it's the rumor that I'm some kind of queer, then you're a little late on that one."

"Don't make this harder for me, Shel."

"Sorry.

---

[165] There is no problem so small that you can't make it a million times worse by imagining dramatic catastrophes.

"There's this guy, Duncan ..."

Dammit, Duncan. What have you done?

"... Some guys saw you and him together and he got asked what you were doing together, and he said that you hit on him and he told you to screw off or he'd beat you up, or something like that."

I wanted to tell Jen everything. I wanted to tell her how I didn't even really like him that much, and how we'd had this one weird moment together, and nothing had happened since and wasn't likely to. I *wanted* to tell her that, but how could I? How could I separate the truth from the lies?

"That's all BS," I lied.

"I knew it." I could hear the relief in her voice. "I keep telling people, since when does Shel hang around with Tech Kids?"

Since the Tech Kid was secretly gay.

She asked, "So what really happened?"

"Duncan lives, like, ten houses down from me. We were both cutting class ..."

"Since when do you cut class?"

"Oh, you know, I'm a bad-ass now."

"As if."

"I know. Anyway, we were playing basketball, that's it."

"So you really were hanging out with him?"

"A little bit."

More than just a little.

I added, "He probably made up that stupid story so it wouldn't look like he actually wanted to be around me."

"That sucks. I'm so sorry."

"I can handle it."

"Shel?"

"Yeah?"

"You wanna get together some time? Just hang out and talk or whatever?"

100 bajillion percent yes.

"Sure."

I was in Mr. Aiden's room, playing cards with Mary-Beth, Marta, and Tim. I couldn't concentrate and had to stop the game.

"Guys," I said, "I don't know what to do about this speech thing."

"What do you *want* to do?" Marta asked.

"I don't know. The first time I did it, I felt cornered. It was like a fight or flight thing. I thought I had to do it, just to protect myself. But as soon as I opened my stupid mouth, I got my head kicked in. It seems crazy to do it again, but if I don't, I'm basically letting those guys win."

Andrew, who had been eyeing us from his seat by the window, turned in our direction and asked me, "What are you so worried about?"

"Well, getting beat up again, for one thing."

"But they've been leaving you alone, right?"

"Yeah, for now. It could be even worse next time."

"Or not," Andrew replied, shrugging.

"And pretty much the whole school's going to hate me."

"What do you care if a bunch of jerks hate you? Just do it."

"Easy for you to say."

He gave me a dismissive gesture and turned back to slouching in his seat.

"Asshole," Tim said. I shot him a quick smile.

Good boy, Timmy.

But Andrew's right, in a way. If I didn't care, there wouldn't be a problem.

I thought of everything that had happened since my last speech—Mr. Aiden, the Bastards, Duncan.

I said, "My teacher told me I'm allowed to change the speech a bit. Maybe I could, I don't know, defend myself. Explain things better. Say some of the things I want to say."

"You think that would help?" Marta asked.

"I have no idea."

I put my elbow on the desk and rested my head in my hand. "Honestly, you guys. Would you do it if you were me?"

Marta laughed and shook her head. "Nooooo way! Forget about it."

"Uh-uh," Tim said. Considering that he hardly spoke at all, it was hard to imagine him unloading his deepest secrets in front of a crowd that would almost certainly hate him for it.

Mary-Beth gave her head a series of quick shakes. "Maybe later. In university."

"Oh!" Marta said, and reached into her satchel, pulling out a narrow slip of wrinkled paper. "I forgot to show everyone this."

It read: "Come out! Come out! To the 4th annual Gay

and Lesbian Conference!"[166] It was some event up at the university—information sessions, display booths, a mixer later in the evening.

Leaning in close, Mary-Beth said quietly, "It's in a few weeks."

Marta added, "We're going to tell our parents we need to go to the university library and then check it out."

"Cool," I said, but I couldn't think about all that. Mary-Beth and Marta, they were thinking about their future, but I had too much to deal with in the present to worry about what I was going to do tomorrow.

I stood facing the closed door of my locker. God only knew what was growing inside. The paint had been retouched, but the fresh coat had done little to cover up the jagged impression of the word "faggot." And somewhere, buried within, was my copy of *Tess*.

I'd had the same lock since grade nine and the combo was burned into my brain. I was able to dial it without even thinking about the numbers. When the lock released, I took hold of the door handle but didn't pull it open. Touching my locker was giving me a strange feeling, and not just because of the funky smell coming from inside it. I used to open that door ten times a day; now I carried everything around in

---

166 At one time, this would have just been labeled a "gay" event but the world had moved forward enough to include "lesbian" in things like this. It would still be a little while before the B, T, and Q were commonly added to LGBTQ. These days, you'll sometimes see even more letters, like LGBTTIQQ2SA (Lesbian, Gay, Bisexual, Transexual, Transgendered, Intersex, Queer, Questioning, Two-Spirited, Allies), and so on, in an effort to be even more inclusive. It might seem like a little much, but when you've spent your whole life feeling like you don't belong, it's very empowering to be recognized.

my knapsack. I felt like an archeologist about to open an ancient Egyptian tomb, except the history I was uncovering was my own. I took a deep breath and opened the door. A rotten, sulfuric odor crept into my nostrils.

Please tell me I didn't leave a sandwich in there for a month ...

Littering the base of the locker was a heap of fractured hard-boiled eggs, all in different stages of decomposition. Whoever had done it, and I could guess it was the Bastards, must have crammed them up into the handle and let them fall down. Covering my nose with the back of my left hand, I scanned the interior space.

Twenty rotten eggs and no Tess.[167]

But something did catch my eye: a folded piece of paper. My name was written across in a childish hand. It didn't look like hate mail. I picked it up gingerly.

Dear Shelton,[168]

You don't know me but we met before. I heard about your speech and I am sorry that anybody hurt you or anything. I think you are brave—braver than me because I am sort of like you. You are the first person I have told that to and no one else knows.

P.S. Please burn this when you have read it so that no one sees my handwriting.[169]

Judging from the amount of smudgy egg soaking into the

---

167 Tess was eventually found in my bathroom at home. Don't judge me.
168 He almost got it right.
169 I didn't burn it but I did keep it secret. Thanks, whoever you were.

paper, it had been there a few days. I put the letter in my knapsack, pocketed the lock, and shut the door on those rotten eggs.

Chapter Twenty-Four

When I walked into the caf on the day of the school-wide speech competition, the room was already filling up. The stage was ready to go, three chairs to the right, three more to the left, and a podium in the middle. Panic surged through my body and I stopped moving. Students flowed in around me.

I can't do this again.

I got pushed forward by the crowd and began stumbling in the direction of the stage. As I moved toward the front of the caf, I couldn't help but be reminded of the fact that I was walking the same route I had taken on the day when I was running for my life from the Bastards. The situations may have been different, but I was scared then and I was scared now.

At the far corner of the room, I could see Mrs. Piedmont

ascending the short flight of steps leading to the stage. She was holding up the sides of her dress to keep from tripping. She joined two other teachers and they began to talk.

I was following this girl from my grade, Eva, who was heading in the same direction I was. She was skinny and had long black hair. She walked all the way to the stage, climbed the steps, and took a seat. She looked nervous.

Just before I climbed the steps, a voice from beside me said, "Good luck, brother." I turned to see Derek, the janitor, leaning against the wall.

Just one more person about to learn my big secret, I thought. I hoped he wouldn't hate me when I was done.

"Thanks," I said and gave him a tiny wave.

I was using the same index cards I had earlier, but with all kinds of changes scrawled over them in red. They'd become soggy from the sweat of my hands. I held one by the tips of my fingers and waved it like a white flag, hoping to dry it off before it fell apart completely.

I took the stairs slowly, not wishing to hurry toward the moment when I'd have to spill my guts to this whole crowd. I sat down in a chair beside Eva.

I did this before, I told myself, *I can do it again. And it had worked, too. No one's given me a hard time since. Well, except for the time I got my head split open and was left for dead ... But that won't happen again, right?*

It was hot on the stage. Once again, I'd worn a long-sleeve shirt over my AC/DC tee. I unbuttoned the over shirt so I wouldn't sweat, but I still wasn't ready to take it off completely. Besides, anyone who looked close enough could probably figure out what I was wearing.

Students continued to fill the cafeteria. The reality of what I was about to do was overwhelming. Forget butterflies in the stomach, I had rhinos. I needed some way to *not* think about it. I looked over at Eva. She held a small set of blue index cards in her hand.

"Hi," I said.

"Hi," she replied.

"Nervous?" I asked.

"Yes," she replied, tight-lipped.

"What's your speech about?"

"My Ukrainian heritage," she answered. It was clear she didn't want to talk. Which I was kind of glad of, actually. What would I have said if she'd asked me about mine?

She'll know soon enough, anyway.

From the far side of the stage, another classmate, David, came toward us. I guessed he was the final contestant. He was kind of stocky, with a buzz cut. In his hand he held a piece of paper that was folded in thirds like a letter.

"Hey," I said.

He sat down heavily and nodded. He unfolded his speech. Out of the corner of my eye, I could see that it was typed. My note cards, damp and covered in an illegible scrawl, looked sad by comparison.

A thin, bearded teacher named Mr. Woods went up to the podium and spoke into the microphone.

"OK, if everyone could take their seats ..." His request went largely ignored as students took advantage of the rare opportunity to chat during class time.

"Everyone ..." he went on. "*Please* take your seat."

At the front of the caf, a guy stood up and turned to the noisy throng.

"SHUT UP!" he yelled, his low voice booming out over the hubbub. This was greeted with a mixture of laughter, hooting, and applause. The room settled down.

Mr. Woods said, "Thank you. Welcome to the annual speech finals. Please listen closely to the excellent examples of public speaking you're about to hear. You'll be voting on them when we get back to class. And I expect you *all* to return to class at the end of the speeches. Anyone who doesn't will be marked absent. Understood?"

I looked over at Mrs. Piedmont. She was seated beside another teacher, a woman of about the same age but lean, with heavy jewelry and long gray hair.[170] They were chatting quietly. Mrs. Piedmont looked over at me and waved.

I thought, *I wouldn't be up on this stage if it weren't for her*.

But I wasn't sure if that was a good thing or bad.

"First up," Mr. Woods said, "is David Money ..." A loud and boisterous burst of whoops and hollers rang out from a small group at the front of the stage.

Well, I guess I know who they're voting for ...

"... Settle down, settle down." The teacher said. "David was selected from my class and will be reading from his speech, 'Sports and Scholarly Achievement.'"

Another round of cheering.

"From Mrs. Piedmont's class, we have Sheldon Bates

---

170 We had some "groovy" teachers who were holdovers from the hippie era. Peace, man.

reading his speech ... which doesn't seem to have a name here ...

I didn't know it was supposed to have a name. I'd never given it one.

Maybe I should have called it "ac/dc." Then everyone would have thought it was about the band, at least until I started talking.

Actually, that's a bad idea.

"... and from Ms. Beier's class we have Eva Ku ... Ku ..."— he struggled with the name—"... Kuchin? ... and her speech, 'What My Baba Taught Me.'

"So, without further ado, please put your hands together for David Money."

The teacher took a few steps back, clapping for David, who pushed himself to his feet and stepped slowly to the podium. When he got there, he set his paper down in front of him and ran a hand through his short hair. Sweat was standing out on his pink face.

"Hey," he said to the crowd. He wiped his forehead with the back of his hand. "It's frickin' hot up here."

He looked down at his sheet and began to read.

"Sports are important to schools for a number of reasons." He paused to clear his throat, keeping his place on the page with a thick finger. "Sorry. So, yeah, sports are important to scholarly achievement for a number of reasons. One of these reasons is health. Sports exercise your body and improve your health. So, if you went out for two rugby ..." The small group at the front roared. David looked out at the crowd and whispered, "Rugby rules."

This was met by a boisterous round of good-natured booing and choruses of "Football rules!"[171]

"Football's gay," David said, and the audience roared with laughter.

There was no question about it. He may have been nervous, but the crowd loved him, which meant they were probably going to hate me.

Why am I even bothering?

"OK, OK, settle down."

I saw David looking for his spot on the page. "Where the hell was I? Oh, right. OK. So, if you went out for two rugby practices and one game a week, you'd get more than the doctor-recommended amount of exercise. People who exercise are sick less often and miss less school and so they get better grades. When you look at it like that, sports are important to scholarly success."

As he talked, I began to zone out, preoccupied with the thought that in a few short minutes it would be me up at that podium.

I can get up and leave right now.

My knee started bouncing around like crazy.

No. Relax. Do not chicken out. Not now.

Applause rang out through the caf. I looked up to see David lifting his hand in a casual gesture to the crowd. He came back to his chair and sat down. His face was bright red and sweating.

"Good job," I said.

"Thanks," he replied.

---

171 Witness the eternal struggle between football and rugby.

The emcee waved, indicating it was my turn. My heart sank into my stomach and part of my brain started screaming at me to walk right off the stage. But somehow, I managed push past it. I stood up and walked over to the podium, my legs shaking, an invisible fist clamped around my throat. The stage lights were so bright that I could hardly see the audience, which was kind of a mercy.

Here we go ...

"Hi. A little while ago, because of something that happened to me, I thought that I was gay."

I stopped to take a breath. I felt like throwing up, but I'd made it past the first word, which was better than last time. From multiple places in the audience, I heard the word "faggot" buried within a series of bogus coughs.

Just keep going ...

"So. So this was scary for me, as you can imagine. Then I realized that I wasn't just gay, I was bisexual, which means being attracted to both girls and guys. It was a secret, but then some other people found out about it.

"Since then, I've had some people stop being friends with me."

Sarah.

"Some people wanted to be my friend, but didn't know how to. Or, for whatever reason, I just didn't let them."

Dan.

"Some people needed time."

Jenny.

"Some people have made false accusations against me, people who should have known better."

Duncan.

After that, I continued on automatic pilot, talking without thinking. I kept my eyes on my notes, occasionally looking up at the bright lights shining over the audience.

When I came to some more new material, I began to refocus on what I was doing.

"There are people in this school who have threatened to hurt me, who *have* hurt me, just because of who I am. I don't deserve that. No one does."

I became aware of tinkling noises around me and saw that coins were being flicked on to the stage. Muffled laughter burbled up from the audience and I felt my blood rise.

From the corner of my eye, I saw Mr. Woods get up from his seat and step down from the stage.

"These people hurt me to try and stop me from doing what I'm doing right now, which is telling the truth."

A ball of paper came out of nowhere. Because of the bright lights, I didn't see it until the last minute. It struck my shoulder and bounced off. More laughter came from the audience, and I boiled with anger and frustration and humiliation.

I saw Mr. Woods hurrying below me. Voices began to rise from the crowd, and I raised my own voice to make sure I was heard above them.

"If they try it again, I promise I'll be right back up here." I jammed my finger onto the top of the podium to emphasize my point.

Something I couldn't quite make out was happening beyond the glare of the lights. I could hear agitated voices and the sound of seats scraping against the floor. Not knowing what else to do, I just kept going, even though I was sure that only half of the audience was even looking at me.

"Since this all came out, I've been called every name in the book. One person called me Switch, which I don't even mind. If you have to call me something, I guess it can be that. The last thing I want to say is that some of you out there are gay or bi. I hope you're all OK."

I set my cards down and looked up, squinting into the bright lights. There was a scuffle in the far aisle. It was hard to see, but it looked like Mr. Woods and Derek were dragging a student away, his angry voice ringing back and forth across the large room. Everyone in the audience was talking at once. How much was about me and how much was about the kid who got kicked out I wasn't sure. I walked back to the side of the stage and collapsed in my chair.

David Money shook his head in a gesture of total disbelief. "Jesus Christ, dude. You're crazy."

"It sure looks that way," I replied.

I got calls from both Dan and Jen that night. Dan's was just a short check-in, but Jen and I talked for a while.

"That was crazy," she said.

I knew what she meant. Not many high school speeches end in a near riot. Plus, I'd basically dared the Bastards to try it again.

"I know. It was kind of stupid."

"Not crazy-*stupid*, like, crazy-*brave*."

"It doesn't feel brave; it feels insane."

"Well, whatever. It took guts. You did great. I'm sorry everyone was so rude while you were talking."

"Thanks."

"You think you'll win?"

"Unlikely. I hope Eva does. Hers was the best."

"Yeah, but you know how these things go. You could have the best speech in the world but it's all a popularity contest. Dave Money has it in the bag."

"Probably."

"Well, if I had my way, you'd win."

"Thanks."

"Who was that girl in the army coat who hugged you when you came off the stage?"

"I have no idea."

"That's weird. Maybe coming out will help you pick up girls."

"Ha! I doubt it. So far it's just that one girl, and she smelled like a barn."

We chatted for another half an hour or so, then made a plan to meet up that weekend. After we hung up, I began to wonder: Is it too much to think that maybe we really could get back together again?[172]

In Room 115 at lunch the next day, I thought that I might get a hero's welcome, or at least what passed for one with the crew we had. But the only one there was Mr. Aiden. I wondered if they all felt like they had to distance themselves

---

172 Yes.

from me now. Could I blame them if they did?

"Where is everyone?" I asked Mr. Aiden.

"I'm not sure, Sheldon. Probably just held up. Are you happy with how your speech went?"

"Happy it's over, anyway."

"Well, I thought you did quite well, despite the behavior of some members of the audience. I know it couldn't have been easy for you. It was truly a brave thing you did."

"Truly stupid, more like it."

"Don't say that, Sheldon. You don't know how much your speech might mean to someone in the audience."

I spent the rest of that lunch eating and reading in silence. Shortly before the period ended, Marta, Mary-Beth, and Tim arrived, with Andrew strolling in behind them.

"Where were you guys?" I asked.

"Nowhere," Marta and Mary-Beth blurted out in unison.

"Right. Nowhere," Andrew said, rolling his eyes. He took a seat. Tim slunk off to the back of the room.

Shortly before the bell rang that day, the amused voice of Tyler, our Head Boy,[173] came buzzing out of the PA system.

"Hello, one and all. Before you make your escape for the day, I want to tell you who will be representing our school ..." He stopped as laughter began to overtake him. "... at the regional speech finals. The winner is ..." He could barely speak he was laughing so hard. "... Sheldon Bates, AKA Switch ..."[174] His voice became a tight, hysterical squeak as he said, "Congratulations and good luck!" There was a rattle

---

173 The male student body president. There's also a Head Girl.
174 I did ask for it, after all.

and a click, and then the PA system went silent. The whole class turned toward me.

I looked over at Dan but all he did was shrug.

Without even knowing what I was saying, I mumbled, "That's impossible."

"It *was* a very powerful speech," Mrs. Piedmont said.

Kelly was furious. "Better than the one that Ukrainian girl did? She didn't look at her notes once, and I saw a teacher actually *crying* by the end of hers."

I knew what Kelly was implying, that I must have cheated somehow. And I had to admit, I could see her point. There was no way the majority of the school would ever vote for me.

My first thought was that it was all some kind of conspiracy, just like in Stephen King's *Carrie*. I'd show up for the big speech finals and the Bastards would drop a bucket of pig's blood on my head. But then the truth finally hit me, and I realized where everyone had been at lunch. I couldn't believe I hadn't figured it out earlier.

Kelly was right. I *had* cheated. Or, more accurately, someone had cheated for me. While I was sitting alone in Room 115, the rest of my crew were out counting ballots, and making sure that I came out on top.[175]

The next day at lunch, I marched into Room 115, ready to confront my friends about rigging the vote. I thought I was done with speechmaking, but now, because of them, I was being asked to do it all over again.

---

175 So, yeah. They committed electoral fraud. Totally the wrong thing to do, but it was for a good cause.

When I entered the room, Andrew looked up from a novel he was reading. "Our hero," he said with a smirk.

Mr. Aiden said, "Congratulations, Sheldon."

I'm sure I didn't do a very good job of covering up my irritation when I said, "Thanks."

I pulled a chair up to the table where Mary-Beth and Marta were sitting.

In an angry whisper, I asked them, "Why did you do that?"

"Do what?" Marta asked.

"C'mon," I said, "I know you did it."

They looked at each other, realizing they'd been found out.

Sheepishly, Marta said, "We wanted to help you win."

"Yeah, but I didn't *really* win."

Marta added, "Plus, Mary-Beth had the idea that if everyone thinks that everyone *else* voted for your speech, maybe they'll change their attitude about you."

It was nice to know that my friends cared so much, and I had to be impressed by Mary-Beth's devious plan,[176] but still.

"You should have asked me first."

Mary-Beth said quietly, "We thought it would make you happy."

Tears were welling up in her eyes and I started to feel like an unappreciative jerk.

"Guys, I know you meant well. But I haven't even told my parents yet, and now I'm supposed to do it in front of the whole town."

---

176 Sometimes it really is the quiet ones.

Marta asked, "You've already done it twice. Third time should be easier, right?"

I put my elbows on the desk and pushed my palms against my eyes. "I have no idea."

Chapter Twenty-Five

Jen stepped out of her doorway and into the amber glow of the late-afternoon sunlight. Her face lit up and she looked so perfect, so beautiful, it was almost like she'd planned it just to amaze me.

"You want to go for a drive?" she asked.

"Sure. Where you want to go?"

"I don't know. Anywhere that my mom can't eavesdrop on us."

"Oh. I guess she doesn't like me, huh?"

Jen lowered her voice to a whisper. "When I told her you were coming over, she said, 'You're not getting back together with HIM again are you?'"

"Hey! I thought she liked me."

She laughed. "Seriously?"

I shrugged. I guess I missed something along the way.

We walked along the gravel drive toward my parents' car, which I'd parked on the roadside. She was quiet, her hands stuffed into the pockets of her cardigan. I opened the passenger door for her, then went around to the driver's side.

"Where to, milady?" I asked.

"Doesn't matter. But before we go anywhere, I've got a little surprise for you." She handed me a small black object.

It was a short cylinder, like a spool, but made of hard plastic.

I turned it over in my hand. "What is it?"

She took it from me and slid it over the bare metal post that had been sticking out from the front of the car stereo, ever since she'd thrown the tuning knob out the window on the night we'd broken up. It went home with a click.

I said, "That's awesome! My parents are going to love you. How'd you ever find it?"

"Duh. It's not the same one, obviously. I got it from a car stereo place."

"Oh." That made sense, considering that the original was lost in a ditch somewhere. "I can't believe it fits."

"I just told them what kind of car it was. They didn't even charge me anything for it."

"No doubt they were hypnotized by your sexiness."

"Omigod," she said, laughing. "You have *the* worst come-on lines on Earth."

"Hey, they worked on you."

She started to say something more but stopped.

"What?" I asked.

"I'll tell you later," she replied.

"OK ... I have something for you, too." I reached into my pocket and gave her two photos from the set we'd taken that last night together.

"Awww," she said. "I forgot about these."

"I've been holding on to them," I said. "I kept the other two. I hope that's OK. One of them is mostly just your jean jacket."

"Is it even worth keeping?"

"Yeah ... sentimental value."

"That's sweet."

I started the engine and headed off. A few minutes later, we were meandering down some wooded back roads. Jen said, "So ... you won the speech contest. I did not see that coming, no offence."

"None taken."

"I guess more people are on your side than anyone thought."

I didn't have the heart to tell her the truth, or the guts to let her know that she'd fallen for Mary-Beth's cunning plan.

She asked, "Who was it giving you a hard time?"

"Just some jerks at school."

"And they hurt you?"

"I had to get some stitches. I'm fine. They've been leaving me alone. I don't really want to talk about it anymore."

"What are we going to talk about then?"

"You."

"Me? God, why?"

"You missed school for a while."

She was quiet for a moment before saying, "Not everything is about you, Shel."

"Really? I thought I was the center of the universe."

"Ha! Not even a little bit."

"I suppose so. But I *was* worried about you."

"I was fine. I *am* fine."

"Are you sure?"

"God, yes. Drop it."

I glared at her, trying to will her to tell the truth.

"Fine," she said. "The main thing was, and I'll spare you the details, I just wasn't feeling great. Like, physically."

"What ..."

"Don't even ask. But also, if I had one more person ask me if I was OK, I was going to lose my mind."

"Oh."

"And that's why I didn't want to tell you, because I didn't want you to feel worse."

"Sorry."

"It's all right."

I looked over at Jen. "I miss you."

"I miss you, too," she said, a little agitated. "You know we're not getting back together again, right? I know it's kind of obvious, but I need to make sure I say it."

Damn.

"Oh, yeah, of course."

"We were going to be broken up soon anyway."

We were?

It didn't make any sense. The last time the two of us were in a car together, we were about to go all the way.

"But I thought we were, you know ..."

"I know," she said, cutting me off. "I think that's why I was so grumpy that night. I kind of knew it was over. I thought we could have this nice moment together and then that would be it. I guess I was mad you couldn't see it."

I had no clue that she had been ready to end it.

"Really?"

"You're a great guy, Shelly, but it was over."

I was about to present evidence to the contrary, when she held up a hand to stop me. "Hold on," she said. When she spoke again, her voice had lost some of its composure. "I've had so many shitty relationships ... and I felt like I was getting hurt all over again. And I treated you like crap ..." Her voice trailed off and she started to cry. "And I'm really sorry."

She cried quietly for several minutes.

I kept driving, trying to get all the pieces of her story to work together in my head.

Eventually I said, "It's not your fault, Jen. I shouldn't have dropped it on you like that. It was really bad timing."

"Ha!" she said, her voice quavering. "I bet you're kicking yourself that you didn't wait until after we'd done it."

"You have NO idea."

We laughed together. I made a long, left-hand turn through a stand of dark green trees.

I couldn't stop thinking of what she'd said, about our relationship being terminal. "You were really gonna break up with me?"

"I think so."

"Was there someone else?"

"No! And there hasn't been since, either. I'm kind of off guys for a while."

"Me, too," I said, and we laughed again.

"You know we weren't going to be together forever, right?'

"I don't know ... I loved you. I thought you loved me, too."

"I did love you, but we're just ... different."

"Because I'm bi?"

"I don't know. Maybe. But I'd decided about us before I even knew. We're just ... different. Our lives are going to be different."

"How?"

"Like, do you want to have a really big family with lots of kids?"

"I can't imagine having kids. I can barely look after myself."

"I want kids," she replied. "Lots of them. Do you want to stay in the 'burbs or do you want to move into a city?"

"I don't know. I like it where you live."

"Ugh. There's nothing to do there. And we're so far out, we can't get cable. I want to be around *people*."

"People are overrated."

"Very funny." She turned away from me, looking out her window at the passing fields. "And do you think you could go your whole life with just one person. You know, with, like, 'just' a girl or 'just' a guy?"

I'd certainly asked myself that. But didn't everyone have to figure that question out, or something like it?

"I don't know. I think so."

Some time and many miles later, I pulled up to a secluded section of waterfront and pointed the nose of the car at the sun, which was lowering across the lake. It was a lot more picturesque than the old factory we used to make out behind. We climbed out and sat on the warm hood, our legs dangling off the end. We picked up some little rocks and were throwing them into the water. I asked her about Sarah.

"I don't really hang around with her anymore."

"Why not?"

"Let's just say, she's not the friend I thought she was."

"Like how?"

"Y'know, Shelly, when people say, 'Let's just say,' that usually means they don't want to get into it."

"OK, never mind."

Suddenly she blurted out, "Do you know she has a thing for, y'know, 'pleasuring' guys while they're driving?"

"Isn't that dangerous?"

"Probably." She laughed and looked at her feet. "Omigod. Telling you that is officially the bitchiest thing I've ever done."

"Sarah? Really? I can't imagine anyone being able to tolerate her long enough to get that far."

"Guys will put up with just about anything to get what they want."

"I guess. That's weird."

"Normally, I'd say, 'Don't tell anyone,' but what do I care? Tell anyone you want."

"Wow. I've never seen you this pissed off before. At someone besides me, anyway. It's kinda sexy."

She laughed. "You're funny. I think I forgot about that. I'm going to miss you when you go away to university next year."

"We can stay in touch," I suggested.

"Sure," she replied, but I wasn't convinced she meant it. "So, you're really going to do your speech at the city finals, huh?"

"You know, when people say they don't want to talk about something ..."

"C'mon, Shelly."

"Honestly, I don't know if I'm going to do it. Part of me wants to just bail. It's like, why even bother?"

"I think it would be an incredibly brave thing to do."

"I'm tired of being brave."

"Yeah, I bet."

I said, "But if I do decide to do it, you can come if you want. They saved me a few seats for guests. I just have to put your name down."

"What about your parents? Won't they need them?"

"Uh ..."

"Omigod, you *still* haven't told them? How is that possible? The whole world knows!"

"It just hasn't been a good time."

"They are going to *freak out* if they hear it from someone else."

"They're going to freak out, regardless."

"You know what I mean."

"Yeah, yeah. I don't wanna think about it. I told Bill, though."

"And he hasn't told them?"

"No. I don't think so, anyway."[177]

"How'd it go with him?"

"Marginally better than with you. I didn't end up with a bruise afterwards."

"Sorry about that."

"That's OK. I deserved it."

Her tone changed abruptly, becoming deadly serious, "Don't say that."

"Say what?"

"Don't say you deserve to be hurt because that's NEVER true."

"Whoa, where'd that come from?"

"Oh ... I'm going to a therapist. Not about you. Well, partly. Mostly I just have a lot of crap to work through. It's kind of cool, actually. Now I write everything down instead of letting it drive me crazy. My therapist says that when you write something down, part of your bad thoughts crawl out your ear, down your arm, and onto the paper. You should try it."[178]

"Maybe. I don't think my parents would go for sending their kid for therapy, though."

"They would if you convinced them that you needed it. Like, maybe by ... coming out to them," Jen said with a smile.

"Jeez, you don't give up."

"Nope."

"OK, I will. I promise. But *after* my speech."

---

177 As I learned later, Bill actually had told them. But, thankfully, he asked them not say anything until I told them myself, which I did, eventually.
178 That you're reading this is proof that I took her advice.

"You swear?"

"I swear. Cross my heart, hope to die, stick a needle in my eye."

"Good." I looked into her eyes and she smiled so sweetly, I thought my heart might crumble. She said, "Shelly, I'm going to give you one kiss and it's going to be a really nice moment, and then it'll stop and we'll just be friends, OK?"

I nodded.

"Then I've got to go home before my mom calls the cops."

She leaned toward me and touched her soft lips against mine. After a long moment together, I pulled away, and began kissing her neck.

"Shelly?"

"Mm-hmm?" I mumbled, my face pressed into her shoulder.

"You're wrecking our nice moment."

I stopped kissing her and sat upright once again. "Sorry."

Smiling, she said, "It's nice to see some things never change."

I pulled over in front of her house and said, "I'll let you know about the speech and save you a seat if you want."

She said, "OK, see ya," and climbed out of the car. I was hoping for more of a goodbye.

Before she could close the door, I said, "Hey, Jenny?"

"Yeah?" she said, leaning in.

I was thinking about what she'd said about Sarah, and how Dan had always denied being a couple with her.

"What's the deal with Sarah and Dan?"

"What do you mean?"

"Y'know, were they, like, secretly going out, or what?"

"Are you kidding me? Why do you think Dan always wanted to drive her home?"

"Seriously?"

"Seriously. You didn't know that?"

"Dan always said nothing was going on."

"Well, he would."

"But I asked you and you said the same thing."

"She was my friend. I had to. God, Shelly. How can someone so smart be so dumb?"

"I don't know. Why didn't they just go out?"

"Uh ... Because they hate each other?"

"But then why would they ..."

She cut me off. "You have a lot to learn about people, Shelly."

Chapter Twenty-Six

Room 115 was usually kept in a state of welcoming half-shadow, but when I arrived for lunch, it was brightly lit. A number of desks had been knocked out of place and their chairs tipped over. Mary-Beth and Marta were there, visibly shaken, and trying to put the room in order.

"What's going on?" I asked, guessing at the answer, not wanting to hear it.

Marta's face had gone deep red. "Some guys jumped Timmy."

"Where is he?"

"I don't know. He took off when we got here."

I felt sick.

"Was he OK?"

Marta said, "He had blood on his face and he wasn't

wearing his glasses."

"Here they are," Mary-Beth said, lifting his oversize spectacles from the ground.

I wanted to run, to find him, to tell him not to do anything stupid, but I had no idea where he was. Judging from the mess, he'd put up a fight. I picked up a chair and slammed it on its feet.

I was so furious and worried; my blood felt like lava in my veins.

Room 115 was *our* room, *our* sanctuary, and someone had violated it. It made me nauseous just thinking about it. It was the Bastards, or someone just like them, and they'd spotted Tim—quiet, small, and all alone—and they'd pounced, attacking him in the one place he could feel safe.

The PA system crackled and I heard my name being called down to the office.

Damn.

I asked, "Where's Mr. Aiden?"

Mary-Beth said, "In the office, I think."

A few minutes later, I was sitting in a hard plastic chair outside the vice-principal's office, sweating and fuming. My mind swung wildly between hatred, fear, and guilt. I wanted to kill the guys who'd done it. I was terrified of what might happen to Tim. And over and over I wondered:

How much of it was my fault?

A phone rang on the desk of the nearest secretary. She looked in my direction, holding the receiver to her ear. She nodded in reply to some question, then hung up the phone and gestured me into the vice-principal's office. Warily, I got to my feet and went over to the door.

Pushing it open, I peered into the room. The inside was covered in faux wood paneling. The metal desk was grey and green. Squatting on one end was a boxy computer with a huge monitor. Sitting behind the desk, hands clasped, was the vice-principal. Standing beside him was Mr. Aiden.

The VP gestured for me to sit down.

Calmly, Mr. Aiden said, "I'll leave you two to discuss it." As he left the room, he placed a comforting hand on my shoulder.

The vice-principal cleared his throat.

"Mr. Bates."

"Sir," I replied.

"That was some speech you gave the other day."

Through gritted teeth, I said, "Thanks."

"You made some pretty serious accusations."

I shrugged.

"It reminded me of our earlier conversation, where you claimed that nothing had happened to you."

I didn't know what to say, so I said nothing.

"And now there's been an incident with ..."—he looked at a form in front of him—"... this Timothy Greenlea. Mr. Aiden tells me he's a friend of yours."

"I know him."

"Do you want to help him?"

"Sure."

"Then why don't you tell me who's responsible?"

"I don't know. I wasn't there."

"But you have an idea who it was."

I shrugged again.

"I'm trying to help you here, Sheldon."

I actually considered telling him everything, about the Bastards, what they'd done to me and now to Tim, but I didn't. We had to solve this ourselves.

The vice-principal said, "You haven't done anything wrong. Why are you not helping yourself? Why aren't you helping your friend?"

"Because anything I say to you will only make matters worse."[179]

At the end of the day, I was walking out the Appendix exit when I heard a voice yell, "Shel!"

I stopped and turned to see Dan propping a door open. He gestured at someone inside the school and then trotted in my direction.

He said, "Hey, man. I've been looking all over for you."

"What's going on?"

"Tyler wants to talk to you."[180]

Tyler came through the doors and sauntered over to me. I wanted to ask Dan what this was all about but I didn't have time.

"Hey," Tyler said when he got close.

"Hey," I replied.

He asked, "You had some guys giving you and your

---

179 The unspoken prohibition against snitching is a powerful one. Looking back, I understand why I wouldn't tell anyone, especially this guy, but I kind of wish that I had said something.
180 The Head Boy, in case you forgot. So far, you've only heard him as a voice on the PA system.

friends a hard time, right?"

I shrugged indifferently.

"The vice-principal knows who it is; he just needs you to say who. Then he can get them suspended."

"No way," I said.

Dan asked, "Why not? If these guys are bugging you, then screw them. They deserve it, right?"

Why not? Because in a few days, they'd be right back here, madder than ever.

"It won't make anything better," I replied.

We stood in silence for a moment and then Tyler said, "Whatever, man. I'm just trying to help."

"I gotta go," I said and started walking home.

As I was leaving, I heard Dan say, "Thanks for trying to look out for him."

"Like I give a shit," Tyler said.

Chapter Twenty-Seven

I couldn't face going into Mr. Aiden's the next day. I felt like the room had been poisoned. I met Mary-Beth and Marta and invited them to eat outside with me. We sat in the grass and started talking about Room 115.

I asked them, "How did you guys even find out about Mr. Aiden's room?"

Marta said, "This girl, Lorna. She graduated last year. She told me and I told Mary-Beth."

"Did she have kind of crazy hair? Dyed black?"

"Yeah," Marta said.

"I remember her."

In her quiet voice, Mary-Beth said, "Andrew came from Mr. Aiden's old school. I don't know about Tim."

Our conversation stopped at the mention of his name. I'm sure we were all asking ourselves the same questions:

Where is he?

Is he ok?

Could I have done more?

"I can't believe anyone would hurt him," Marta said. "He's the most harmless guy I ever met."

"That's *why* they were able to hurt him," I replied.

Marta looked like she was about to start crying. "It's so stupid. The worst I ever got was being called dyke, and that's mostly 'cause of the ties." She flipped her tie, blue with silver stripes, between her fingers.

Later, as we were packing up our lunch stuff, Marta asked, "You still up for going to that thing at the university?"

I'd forgotten all about it. "That's tonight?"

"Yeah, we're going."

Mary-Beth corrected her. "Well, I don't know for sure. It's up to my parents."

I thought about going. It wasn't like my social calendar was packed, and as much as I liked the kids in the lunch club, all except for Andrew, that is, they weren't anything like my old friends. We didn't hang out or go to parties or anything like that. Maybe I could meet some new friends there, or possibly someone who was more than a friend. The idea was tempting.

I asked, "What do you wear to something like that?"

Marta perked up and said, "I'll just wear this. You should go to the secondhand shop downtown; that's where I get my stuff. Andrew buys his clothes there, too, even if he won't admit it."

A few hours later, I walked into the university's sunlit commons. It was full of people milling around display tables. I checked out a booth and found myself staring at a shockingly graphic safe sex display. When I looked away, I saw two women holding hands. I'd never seen stuff like this in public. It was all so much, so ... open. I wasn't sure whether to be overjoyed or embarrassed.

My new clothes weren't helping me feel more at ease. I'd taken Marta's advice and hit the secondhand clothing shop after school. It wasn't like I could afford anything else, anyway. I was surprised to find that I actually liked the place. It was kind of like that old department store I liked, but less depressing. It was packed with university students.

I set out to recreate Andrew's look, hoping that he wouldn't choose that moment to stop in at the store; if he thought I was imitating him, I'd never hear the end of it. After some time spent poking around, I put together a reasonable recreation of his look: light blue jeans, polo shirt, and penny loafers (no socks). There was no denying my outfit was sharper than what I normally wore, but I felt conspicuous, like I was wearing a costume.

On my way out of the store, I'd picked up a satchel. For weeks, I'd been lugging all my school stuff around in a grubby old knapsack. The satchel cost more than I wanted to spend, but I figured that if I had to carry everything with me for the rest of my life, at least I could do it in style. Outside the store, I switched everything over to the shoulder bag and stuffed my empty knapsack in a garbage pail.

At the conference, despite any misgivings I had about the

way I looked, I tried to play it cool as I checked out the other booths, all the while keeping an eye out for my friends.[181]

I felt weird being there by myself. Everyone seemed to be part of a couple or a group of friends. I was the only loser walking around on my own. I was feeling more and more out of place, getting ready to just give up and go home, when someone caught my eye.

He was my age, I guessed, or maybe just a bit older. I felt an immediate and intense attraction toward him. He wasn't like any of the other guys I'd had crushes on. He was younger, for a start. His hair was sun-bleached blond and his skin the light brown tone of wet summer sand. He was laughing with a gang of girls, checking out the booths. He wasn't like anyone I'd known before. My instincts told me he was gay or bi, but he seemed so *happy*. When he smiled, his whole face beamed. It made me want to be around him.

I started following him from a distance.[182] I tried to be casual, keeping an eye out for where he was, wondering the whole time if I had the courage to talk to him. He stopped at that safe sex booth and picked up a string of about twenty condoms. Someone said something I couldn't hear, then he and his friends all laughed. He dropped the condoms back into the bowl.

I decided to get a little closer. I maneuvered around the room until I was only a few steps behind him. I could hear his voice, which was sweet and warm. I hadn't really expected it to happen, but I was having a crush on a guy, on *this* guy, a guy my own age and right there in front of

---

181 They never showed. I was able to drive myself to campus; they weren't.
182 I realize that I often sound like a creepy stalker.

me. He looked in my direction and we made eye contact. I panicked and knelt down, pretending to tie my shoes. When I felt braver, I looked up and he was gone. I hurried around the commons, hoping against hope that I would find him again, but I didn't.

When I'd first seen him, something had lit up inside of me. Then, just as quickly, that light had been snuffed out. I didn't even know him, but I felt a terrible, inexplicable sadness to think I would never see him again.[183]

I turned toward a nearby table, its top covered by a three-paneled display unit. I buried my face into the space it created, my hands clamped firmly on the rough edge of the table.

My throat became tight.

What is wrong with me?

I didn't get a chance to answer my own question, as I was cut short by an amused voice saying, "Do you have a special interest in menstrual politics?" I looked up at the display I was standing in front of. I was surrounded by more information on the social and political implications of periods than I had ever seen before.[184]

I turned to see who was talking to me. She was tall, almost as tall as me. Her skin was pale, and her strawberry-blonde curls were cut short, encircling her head. Her neck was long and elegant, her intelligent face smiling. She seemed to take an immediate interest in my wellbeing.

She said, "Sorry, I left my display to go pee. Are you all right?"

---

183 But I did! Only it was months later.
184 Which wouldn't have been hard, as I hadn't seen any before that.

"Yeah." Then, for some reason I can't explain, I corrected myself. "Actually, not really."

With genuine sincerity, she asked, "Would you like a hug?"

"Yes," I said. In fact, there was nothing I wanted more at that moment. "I would really, really like that."

She took me in her arms and held my face to her pale, bare shoulder.

She smelled like oranges.

As we held each other, she said, "Did you just get this shirt at the secondhand store?"

What? Is she psychic?

I broke our embrace, wondering how she knew.

She reached around to the back of my collar. "See? It still has the tag on it."

I was mortified. Not only was I walking around wearing a clothing tag, but it was from a secondhand store.[185]

"I love that place," she said and ripped the tag off.

Over Styrofoam cups of water, I quickly summarized how I'd come to be there. I told her about Jen and Sarah, about Mr. Aiden and the lunch club, and the speeches. The whole time, I was thinking:

She's out of my league.

She's beautiful.

She's in university.

And she's hanging around the Gay and Lesbian Conference

---

185 It would still be a few years until grunge would hit and secondhand fashion would be all the rage once again. But at that time, at least in my little world, wearing used clothes basically meant that you were poor.

so she's probably not interested in me.[186]

I realized that I was going on and on about myself. I stopped and asked her more about herself.

"Do you go to the university?" I asked.

She said, "No, I'm still in high school."

Score one, I thought happily.

"One of my mothers works here. She asked me to work the booth."

one of her mothers?

"Your stepmom?"

"No, my parents are both women. They're lesbians."[187]

I was flabbergasted. I tried to come up with a sophisticated reply but was too shocked to speak.

With practiced good nature, she interrupted my awkward attempt to form words. "It's really not that strange. Trust me, some of their parenting ideas are way weirder than the fact that they're both women."

"Like what?"

"Oh, a million embarrassing things." She turned a little red and picked up her cup. She took a sip, her hazel eyes smiling over the rim.

I realized I hadn't told her my name. I reached my hand across the table, "I'm Sheldon."

She reached her long hand out and gave me an amused and formal little shake. "Olympe."

"Olympia? Like, Zeus and all that?"

---

186 Note that, despite being the victim of many an incorrect assumption, I had no problems making such assumptions myself. Live and learn, right?

187 As much as I'd like to say that I took this statement with the calm acceptance of a man of the world, I did not. I'd never met a child of gay or lesbian parents before.

With the slightly frustrated air of someone who had done this a thousand times before, she said, "As in Olympe de Gouge, the French playwright and feminist thinker who was executed by guillotine during the Reign of Terror, June 2, 1793."

"I was named after my great-grandfather. Kind of lame compared to yours."

"Well, I think Sheldon's an intriguing name. You could be a character in a *fin-de-siècle*[188] novel."

I didn't know what that meant, so I just let it go.[189]

"Some people just call me O," she said.

"So, your parents raised you kind of strict?" I said, changing the topic before we reached the subject of *my* past nicknames.[190]

"I guess you could say Bette and Rose-Marie[191] are strict. I wasn't allowed to watch TV or see any Disney movies. Bette hates them. But I could watch all the Fellini I wanted."[192]

"That's not *so* embarrassing," I said.

"Well ... they're always pushing me to," she altered her voice to take on the tone of a professor, "explore and celebrate my sexuality."

I coughed into my water.

She made a fake puking sound. "Gag."

---

188 "End of the century," specifically, the end of the 19th century. OK, so I was waaaay out of my depth.

189 I had to do that a lot with her. She'd spent so much time with academics, she was already talking like one.

190 My last name was Bates. You figure out what school kids did with that.

191 I could never get used to calling my parents by their first names, but she was raised to it.

192 For a kid, this would not be as much fun as it sounds. Actually, that would be true for most adults.

We both laughed.

"As for my donor father,[193] he lives in the U.S., so I don't see him very much. He was one of Bette's ex-boyfriends. Bette's my birth mother."

"She dated guys?"

"When she was younger. She really liked Will; that's my donor father. They didn't make it as a couple, obviously, but they stayed in touch."

"That's my brother's name, sort of. He's a William too but everyone calls him Bill."

She said, "Hold on. Is your brother a film professor, about 50 years old, skinny, tall, gray hair, speaks with a Welsh accent?"

"Um ... no."

"That's good, because if my father was your brother, than you're my uncle, and that would make kissing you very weird."

She winked at me and then stretched her arms as I glowed inside.

I thought about the speech that I was supposed to do, and the reasons why I wanted to do it, and the reasons why I didn't. I tried to wrap my tongue around the unusual combination of letters that made up her name.

"Olympe?" I asked

"Mm-hmm?"

"You know that big speech thing that I'm supposed to do?"

She nodded.

---

193 As in, the man who provided one-half of the genetic equation in her conception.

"How'd you like to be my date?"[194]
"Absolutely," she replied.

---

194 In case you're wondering, no, the irony is *not* lost on me that I fell in love with a girl at a gay and lesbian conference.

Chapter Twenty-Eight

The next day, we got the news that Tim was safe and relatively sound. Turned out he'd been saving his money and had taken the bus to Ottawa to stay with relatives. I supposed that was his plan all along, but the attack had sped it up. Mr. Aiden got Tim's new address and sent him his glasses. Even though he wasn't with us, we all felt a tremendous sense of relief just knowing that Tim was OK. Now that we knew where he was, we went back to meeting in Room 115.

When I got in at lunch, I said, "I'm going to do the speech."

"Wonderful," Mr. Aiden said. "I can try to arrange travel for anyone who wants to go."

Mary-Beth and Marta seemed enthusiastic, but Andrew didn't say anything, just kept his nose buried in a magazine.

"Andrew?" Mr. Aiden said.

Andrew looked up from his reading. With as little enthusiasm as possible, he said, "I wouldn't miss it for the world."

That weekend, Olympe and I were strolling hand in hand by the water, making our way back to her beautiful old house for dinner. She was asking me questions about my life, and I told her about the time I sat on the floor, rating the passersby.

"But your methodology was flawed," she said. "It was based solely on appearances. What about all of the other, you know, elements to attraction?"

More defensively than I would have preferred, I said, "Like what?" For some reason, I felt protective of my little experiment.

She gestured dramatically with her hands as she spoke. "Where's the magic when two people meet? Or how about falling in love with ... I don't know ... someone's voice? Or the way they smell? What about the ... *je ne sais quoi?*"[195]

"I guess I never made it that far."

"But think about it. If I asked you which qualities you find attractive in someone, would they all be physical?"

I took a moment to ponder her question, and then replied, "No, you're right. But you know what's weird? I always had crushes on girls in my class but never any of the boys."

"But you said that you did have guy crushes, right? But they were usually older?"

I nodded.

---

195 Literally, "I don't know what" but used to describe an indescribable something. Not surprisingly, her French was *incroyable*.

"That's not so weird. Everyone has 'types.' That's your type."

"I guess so." But then there was that blond guy I saw at the conference. He was something different.

She said, "I think it's amazing that you were able to bury your attraction to guys for so long, until that day in the pool. Because it's not like sexuality is a ... you know ... a light switch that can be flipped off and on."

It felt good to be able to talk to someone so openly about stuff like this, but our conversation was getting a little beyond what I was comfortable with.

"I'm sorry," she said, "I'm treating like you a test subject. My mothers do that to me and I hate it. They want to make sure that I'm not oppressed or anything, so they're always asking me questions and encouraging me, and it all drives me crazy. Like when I was twelve, they put me in this wretched computer camp because they think we need more girls in the sciences. I mean, we do, but *please*. Computer camp?"

I was still thinking about what she'd said about types. "What kind of guys do *you* like?" I asked.

"Well, I *absolutely* have this thing for French artists and writers." She touched her free hand to my arm. "Proust, definitely.[196] If he wasn't gay, he would be my number one pick."

"Why?"

"I guess because he seems so brilliant and soulful, and he has this *adorable* mustache."

---

196 Famed French author who wrote a massive semi-autobiographical work *À la Recherche du Temps Perdu*. Also, he was an exemplar of gayness.

She seemed so open and unflappable, I took a chance and asked her, "What about girls?"

"I'm not really attracted to girls, but I do feel like I have a connection to some really strong women, like Proserpine,[197] Angela Davis,[198] Dorothy Parker,[199] Debbie Harry.[200] If I met a girl who was like all of them mixed together, then *maybe* I could be attracted to her. Actually, it would probably just be admiration. But I'd still date her, because our conversations would be amazing."

Dinner was ready when we got back. Before we started, Olympe dimmed the lights, put on some jazz, and lit candles in brass candelabra in the center of the table. I was so out of my element, I was on the verge of nervous collapse the whole time we ate.

Halfway through dinner, Bette asked me, "What are you thinking of for a career?"[201]

"Something with math, I think. Maybe teaching."

"That's great, Sheldon. The world could use more queer teachers."

At her casual use of the word "queer," a piece of eggplant casserole[202] became stuck in my throat and I made an involuntary gagging sound.

---

197 Mythological figure. Olympe had a poster of her in her bedroom, a painting by Rossetti.

198 American civil rights activist.

199 American writer and all-around sarcastic person. She was known to use a phrase along the lines of, "What fresh hell can this be?" whenever her doorbell rang.

200 Super cool singer of the new wave band Blondie. Somehow Olympe knew who she was, despite being raised in pop culture isolation.

201 I had one more year of high school left and was still uncertain.

202 This was the day I discovered how much I dislike eggplant.

Bette asked, "Are you all right?"

I nodded and felt my face turning red. I took a big drink of water.

Bette was serious and round-faced, not like Olympe at all, although they did share the same pale skin and fair hair. Rose-Marie was more gregarious, but also quite on edge, as she had just quit smoking and her nerves were frayed.

"Do you like my eggplant?" she asked, laughing nervously, wiggling a fork between her fingers.

"Yeah, it's great," I said, trying to swallow my last bite.

"I'm going to get Bette off meat if it kills me."

"And I'm never giving up bacon," Bette replied coolly, "so you can forget about it."

When we'd finished dinner, Rose-Marie said, "I'm off to go crazy. Save me lots of dessert." She took about twenty toothpicks from a ceramic holder and went into the backyard.

Olympe leaned over the table and stage-whispered to me, "This is when she would normally have a cigarette. She's trying to replace them with toothpicks, except she chews right through them. And she's an absolute monster for sweets now. Do you want some tea?"

"Sure," I said. Tea after dinner wasn't something my family normally did, but I wanted to fit in.

Olympe began clearing the table.

I pushed back my chair and stood up. "I'll help." I gathered some plates, turned around, and managed to whack myself on the back of my chair. Pain shot up from my groin.

"Oh, dear," said Bette.

I winced. "I'm ок." The embarrassment was almost as bad as the pain.

"We don't get a lot of that around here," Olympe added, giggling.

"о ..." Bette warned.

But Olympe was undeterred. "You know, it *is* possible for a woman to ..."

"Olympe!" her mother said sternly. "You're just trying to be shocking in front of your friend. It's ..." she struggled for the word. "... childish. And beneath you."

"Sorry," she said, and gave me a devilish grin.

I limped into the kitchen with my stack of dishes. Olympe filled the kettle with water and placed it on the stove.

It was a nice house, older, with heavy moldings and exposed brick. The kitchen was warm and sunny, with heavy terra cotta tiles on the floor. The walls were bright yellow, with fine cracks running down them, and a tile mosaic over the sink. The shelves were full of well-worn cookbooks and scraggly plants. A shaggy gray cat named Oskar ("with a к") lumbered underfoot. It was the kind of place I could see myself living in when I was older.

Olympe took down four heavy, hand-made mugs and set them on the counter. She rummaged in a drawer until she came up with a small metal utensil, a pair of tongs with two mesh hemispheres on the end. She made it open and close like a mouth and said, "Chomp chomp chomp!"

I laughed, "It looks like Pac-Man."

She said, "I wouldn't know."[203]

I looked out the window and saw Rose-Marie sitting on a tree stump, chewing on several toothpicks at once. She saw me looking and waved, then grabbed her hair and made a gesture like she was pulling it out from frustration.

I laughed. "Rose-Marie's really losing it out there."

"She's tried before," Olympe said, "but I think she's going to do it this time."

When the kettle boiled and our tea was poured, we carried our steaming mugs through the house and out into the late spring evening. The house was a two-story Victorian red brick, with a wide, covered front porch. She perched on the heavy windowsill and pulled her long legs up, wrapping her arms around her knees.

I sat down beside her and took a sip. It was hot, very hot. I struggled not to spit it out. The taste was foreign to me, but good, sort of like black licorice, but also woody and almost bitter. Nothing like the Red Rose tea I'd grown up on. I blew across the surface of the mug.

On a wooden table beside Olympe was a small battery-operated radio. She flipped it on and a tinny, bittersweet song came out of the radio's single speaker.

"Oh, I absolutely love this song," she said.[204]

I nodded. It was vaguely familiar.

"What station is this?" I asked.

---

203 Who doesn't know Pac-Man? Sometimes I think she overplayed the whole raised-by-intellectuals thing.
204 "Cattle and Cane" by The Go-Betweens, yet another Australian band. There sure were a lot of them at the time. I could list all of the ones I remember, but just go look them up.

"The one at the university," she said. "I love that they play everything."

We watched the cars go by. The trees along the boulevard were bending slightly in the wind.

"You have a really nice house," I said. "I live in the suburbs. It's kind of boring and all the houses look the same."

"I bet the rodents don't outnumber the humans in your house. Oskar's useless and this place is absolutely *crawling* with mice. Plus, I'm pretty sure there's a raccoon living in our attic."

"It *looks* nice, anyway."

"That's sweet of you to say," she said, and closed her eyes, soaking in the sun.

I did the same. I listened to the sound of the wind in the trees, the song on the radio, and the cars passing by. I felt the sunlight on my face. I tasted licorice in my mouth and smelled the earth of her front garden.

Most of all, I sensed the warmth of Olympe sitting beside me. I wanted to use every ounce of poetry I had to tell her how wonderful this moment felt, how I felt more at peace than I had in ages.

"Olympe?" I said with eyes still closed.

"Mm-hmm?" she replied.

"You're awesome."

She peeked over her shoulder, looking through the window and into the house. Seeing that all was clear, she leaned over and placed a kiss lightly on my cheek.

Chapter Twenty-Nine

Jenny whispered in my ear as she hugged me close. "You're going to do great."

"Thanks, Jen."

"I really mean it, Shelly."

She gave me a kiss on the cheek and then sat down in one of the rows. Of the hundreds of seats in the city auditorium, about twelve had been reserved for me.

Dan was standing behind her. "Good luck," he said and took a seat beside Jen.

I watched the people filing into the auditorium. I couldn't believe I was about to do this all over again.

I saw Jen lean over and say something to Dan. I couldn't hear what it was but they both laughed afterwards. Part of me wished I could trade places with him, be the one sitting beside her. Then I saw her place a hand on his knee and I felt a twinge of jealousy.

Just how friendly are they?

I halted that train of thought right in its tracks. I didn't have time to worry about it.

I saw Olympe approach, stepping gracefully down the steps in a short, swishing dress and a bell-shaped hat.[205] She looked incredible.

She gave me a hug and then stepped back to look at me. I was dressed up in the most stylish clothes I could find at the secondhand store: a lavender and gray silk jacket, white shirt, gray bow tie and slacks. I didn't even bother with the AC/DC T-shirt this time.

A little too loudly, she said, "You look absolutely splendid, darling."

"Thanks for coming." Maybe it was her enthusiastic voice, or her somewhat outlandish get-up, but Olympe was attracting a lot of attention from the people around us. I saw Jen peering at her from the corner of her eye.

I walked Olympe over to where my friends were sitting. "Olympe, I'd like you to meet Jen, who I told you about." Jen just waved, but Olympe leaned in and planted a very stylish kiss on each of her cheeks.

Olympe said, "I've heard so much about you!" Jen looked like she was in the beginnings of a state of shock. "You're even prettier than Sheldon said!" She sat down next to Jen. I went back into the aisle to greet anyone else who arrived.

It was awkward, at least for me, to see the two girls together but, within thirty seconds, Olympe and Jenny were leaning

---

205 A "cloche." Popular with flappers and retro fashionistas.

in toward each other and chatting like gossipy sisters. I was both curious and slightly petrified at the thought of what they might be saying about me.

I pulled out my notes, this time transcribed more legibly, and began going over them, but I was too distracted to concentrate.

Further movement caught my eye, and I saw the lunch club working its way toward me. First was Mr. Aiden, who looked more handsome than ever in what was probably his finest suit and tie. Marta had gone all out and bought a tuxedo. She also had on black-rimmed glasses with the lenses popped out.

I said, "Wow, you look sharp!"

"Thanks!" she said.

Mary-Beth, wearing a demure dress, gave me a small wave. Andrew followed behind, looking cool in jeans, sports coat, and a loose scarf.[206] He gave me a bemused smile, which was probably as close as he was ever going to get to being pleasant. He pushed past the two girls, throwing himself down into the furthest seat with a showy thump. I pretended not to notice when he stretched out his legs, setting his calves down on the seat back in front of him.

"Nervous?" asked Mr. Aiden.

I shrugged my shoulders.

"Well, I'd be more worried if you weren't. You're going to do great. We're all really proud of you."

"Thanks," I mumbled.

He clapped me a little awkwardly on the shoulder and

---

206 Way to outdo me, man.

went to his seat. As he passed by, I got a whiff of his cologne and a little knot tightened in my gut.

A voice came over the loudspeaker system and announced the start of the competition. I took a seat between Marta and Olympe. Olympe took my hand and then Jenny's as well. Jenny leaned back and glared at me behind Olympe's head, silently asking: *Who is this crazy person?*

I just shrugged and smiled.

On my other side, I could see that Mary-Beth and Marta had linked their baby fingers, their hands just barely visible. *Were they a couple or just being friendly?*

That was another thing I had no time to think about.

The host came out and introduced himself. He described the evening, and I learned that I was to be third of five. He called up the first contender, who presented "Love Has No Color." It was an anti-racism piece, powerful, and a real crowd pleaser.

I barely paid any attention to the second speech, "The Prophecies of Nostradamus," as my anxiety overrode my ability to concentrate. But before I knew it, my name was called. A chorus of clapping hands called me forth. I got up to my feet and moved slowly toward the stage. I stared up at the bright lights and then down to the judges, where I found Mrs. Piedmont's face smiling up at me.

I was nervous, a little shaky, and a little sweaty, but nowhere near as bad as I had been the previous two times. Maybe it was because the audience were strangers to me, or because I'd had more practice. Or maybe I was simply less afraid.

I made my way to the stage and took the cards out of my jacket pocket, placing them on the podium in front of me.

The lights were even brighter than before, the audience more obscured. I searched the mass of darkened faces before me, eventually finding my group. They waved encouragingly, except for Andrew, who sat slouched down with his arms crossed.

It's not too late, I thought. *No one's making me do this. I can just walk off the stage. Or, better yet, why not just stay here and make something up that won't complicate my life?*

I scrounged around in my brain for a new topic.

What about the days of the week? Sure, it would be stealing from Kelly, but she didn't have to know, right?

Let's see ...

"Each day is named after something mythological except for Tuesday.[207] Sunday and Monday are named after the sun and moon, although I guess they're not really mythological, are they? Wednesday and Thursday are named after Norse gods, but Friday isn't ... no, wait, Friday is, too ... and Saturday means something about somebody famous ..."

That's terrible. How about, "Tuesday really sucks. Why? Uh ... because it's garbage day?"

Oh, crap.

I looked out at the shadowy, expectant crowd and down to the judges. In the wings, the local cable TV station had even set up a video camera.[208]

I didn't *want* to be up there.

---

207 Incorrect.

208 It would be a slow day when a high school speech competition made the news, but the local cable station was always out recording community events.

I didn't *deserve* to be up there.

But I *was* up there.

"Hi," I said. "A little while ago, because of something that happened to me, I thought that I was gay."

When I was done and the polite applause had stopped, I left the stage and walked up the aisle, feeling hundreds of eyes on me. I stumbled back to my row. Mr. Aiden, Dan, Jen, and Olympe all stood, allowing me to get to my seat.

Dan said, "Good job, man."

As I walked by her, Jen made her finger into a gun and winked at me.

Olympe hugged me, planting a kiss right on my lips.

When we parted, I saw Andrew exiting on the far side, pushing past the row of knees.

I sat down and asked Marta, "What's that all about?"

She just shrugged and shook her head.

Chapter Thirty

A few days after my speech,[209] Jenny called me. Her voice had that mix of irritation and amusement that I knew so well. She said, "So, guess who I just talked to?"

"Who?"

"Your crazy new girlfriend."

Uh-oh...

"She just called me up out of nowhere!" she said incredulously. "Like we were best friends!"

"Well, that was nice of her, right?"

"Shelly, do you know what girls usually say when they call their boyfriend's exes?"

"Um ... let's have a threesome?"

"No!" She laughed. "More like, 'You're a total bitch. Stay

_____

209 Sorry to break the bad news to you, but "Love Has No Color" won the day.

away from my man.' Or something stupid like that. You know what she said?"

"Do I want to?"

"Oh, you do, trust me. She said ... wait a sec, let me get this right. She said that she "just *had* to tell someone how much she is simply *loving* 16th century French composers right now.""

I laughed.

Jenny said, "I don't know anything about classical music!"

"Don't look at me. I don't either."

"When she asked for my phone number at your speech, I didn't think she'd actually use it."

"She must like you, I guess. And she really loves the arts. And French guys."

"C'mon, don't you think it's weird that she'd call me?"

"I don't know."

"Here's the best part. I decided to try and be, like, friendly and everything. So I told her I was watching *21 Jump Street*.[210] I asked her which guy she liked best on it, and she said she didn't have a TV."

"Yeah."

"Where'd you find her? In a time machine?"

I laughed. "This one time, I was telling her about the Smurfs, and I asked her how she thought they reproduced, considering, you know, they only have one female, Smurfette, and she was created as part of an evil plot by Gargamel."

"Tell me you didn't say that to her."

---

210 You might know the comedy/action movie remake, but this was the ridiculous original TV series starring Johnny Depp and a cast of hotties.

"Why?"

"Omigod. If you don't know how bad it is to talk to a girl about how cartoons have sex, then I can't explain it to you."

I laughed again and Jen laughed with me.

When we settled down, I asked her a question that had been nagging away at me. "Jen, do you think dating Olympe makes me a copout?"

"What do you mean?"

"Like, am I chicken for having a girlfriend, considering everything that's happened?"

"I don't know," she said. "Do you feel like a copout?"

"Sort of."

She thought about it for a long time and then asked me, "What's the word for a person who goes out with someone who's gay so the gay person can look straight?"

"A beard."

"Right, a beard. So do you really like her or is she your beard?"

"No, I really, really like her."

"Then I guess the question is, did you do all of this so you could have a boyfriend, or so that you could love whoever you want?"

I hadn't thought about it like that. She was absolutely right.

"Thanks, Jenny."

I started swimming again. It was hard, being back there—smelling the chlorine, feeling the wet tiles under my bare feet, getting back in the water. It was like all of my senses were forcing me to recall the guy who'd given me the kiss of life, the one who set everything in motion.

I asked myself: *How different would my life have been if I'd never made that sudden decision?*

But there was no point really thinking about it, because I would never know the answer.

I had changed so much since I'd last been swimming, but everything about the pool felt weirdly unaltered. Rosa was right back on my case, yelling at me about my asymmetrical whip kick. For some reason, she didn't really bug me anymore. I still thought she was hot, though. That hadn't changed.

One evening, I was doing the backstroke, moving rhythmically, using the stained wooden slats of the ceiling to guide my path. My ears were underwater, and the sound of my own breathing was all I could hear. It felt good to be swimming again; it gave me something to do with all of my energy, and also time to think.

I thought about Olympe, and how we were just starting out together on something that I knew was going to be great. We hadn't talked yet about what me being bi meant for our relationship. That was going to be a big conversation, but I think we were both up for it.

I thought about Jen and Dan and what, if anything, was going on between them. I thought about Marta and Mary-Beth, and the hidden intimacy I'd seen them share. I thought about Tim, bewildered and half-broken, taking a bus to a new life. I thought about Mr. Aiden, and what happened after he left school each day. I thought about

Andrew, with his anger and sadness forever seething inside him. I thought about Duncan and about Sarah and about Derek the janitor.

I thought about all of these people and their lives within lives, living in secret worlds that almost no one else knew.

And then, because I was too busy thinking to actually look where I was going, I smacked my head against the end of the pool. [211]

---

211 And that's where it ended. (I'm a sucker for symmetry.) At least, it's where this set of notebooks ended. Of course, real life doesn't just start and then stop, but this seems like a good place to finish. It feels ... complete, I guess.

Photo credit: Trina Koster

AN INTERVIEW WITH THE AUTHOR

Shel is a great character. He feels like a real person, who seems, in his adult life, to be doing okay. Do you think things are easier for men like Shel than they would have been for someone like Mr. Aiden, a gay man at the time Sheldon was a teenager? Do you think things are different for gay and bisexual kids now than they were for characters like Shel and the others in Mr. Aiden's lunchroom?

Thanks, he feels real to me, too. This is a work of fiction, but it does pull from episodes of my own life. I actually did get pushed into the girls' bathroom, cracked my head open, passed out, and was later sent alone to the hospital in an inhospitable cab. But I wasn't assaulted, I was just play-fighting like an idiot.

Homophobia was completely entrenched in the culture that I grew up in. It was very common for me to hear, "God created AIDS to kill fags" or something similar. In *Switch*, the villains, if you want to call them that, aren't even named. Their hatred is systemic, not personal. Attitudes were already changing rapidly by the end of my high school years, and certainly even more by the time I was in university. I've often wondered what would have happened if someone had come out in a big way during my high school years. That idea was one of the launching points for *Switch*.

I wouldn't say that coming out is a cakewalk for anyone, anywhere, at any time, but I do believe that, in general, it's a bit easier now than it was in Shel's era, which was itself easier than Mr. Aiden's. But so much depends on where you live, what your home life is like, your mental health, your religion, and so on. There are certainly more (and better) representations of LGBTQ people in our popular culture now than there were in days gone by, and that's a big plus.

Another thing that has changed is the presence of the Internet. If Sheldon were a teen today, he wouldn't have to risk looking through an old dictionary (in public) in order to learn about himself. He could find it on any of a thousand sites online. The web also offers unprecedented opportunities to connect with people who share your experiences. But, as the saying goes, any tool is a weapon if you hold it right, and the Internet is no exception. Cyberbullying is an insidious thing and we all know the terrible repercussions it can have.

I've visited some GSA's (Gay Straight Alliances) and I never fail to be wowed by the honesty, bravery, humor, and strength of the kids I meet there. It's really quite remarkable. That's why I dedicated this book to them.

I plotted out Shel's life after the events of this story, but didn't actually use that information, except to inform his overall character. Instead, I came to rely on the genial tone of his footnotes to serve as a palimpsest, a message within a message, from which the reader can infer that Shel went on to be a relatively healthy, happy person. I feel like it's important for young people to know that things can all work out, even if, or especially when, your life feels like an utter disaster.

The use of footnotes in a novel is unusual. Why did you decide to use this format, instead of just weaving those words into the body of the text?

I'm intrigued by things that complicate a traditional narrative. I was reading, or at least attempting to read, James Joyce's *Ulysses* while I was working on *Switch*, and I think his fearless experimentation was starting to affect my mind.

I wanted to examine how an individual's perspective is altered by time. In *Switch*, there are the original events (which we never see), then a recollection of those events (the main text), and, later, a reflection on the recollection (the footnotes). Between those three eras, there is plenty of room for Shel's point of view to change. When it came time to think about how to actually represent the idea of multiple perspectives, I went right to footnotes. It's probably because of the untold number of essays and reports I've written in my life.

When teenaged Shel wrote his memoir, he had already lived and learned from his experiences, and yet he wrote it, primarily, from the perspective he had at the time of the original events, when he was less self-aware. When adult Shel wrote his footnotes, he wasn't bound by such things and was free to give away as much as he pleased, such as in the first chapter, when he quickly puts to rest the notion that there will be some kind of romance between Shel and the guy from the pool.

I didn't want to go overboard with the historical nature of the book, but it is set in 1988, and so the footnotes gave me the opportunity to comment on life at that time. Because I'm the same age as Shel, I didn't really have to research the era, I just had to resist the temptation to overload it with the music, movies, and books that I loved at the time. Shel has his own tastes, which, back then, I would have called boring. He would have said I was weird. *C'est la vie.*

You had some other ideas, while working on Switch, **for "things that would be funny or clever or weird," but you decided not to use them. Can you share any of them with readers? Can you say why you opted not to use them?**

Similar to what I said above, I love things that subvert expectations. A good example is when Shel finally gets to a place where he can accept his same-sex attractions, then proceeds to fall in love with a girl. (That may have happened *because* he had accepted himself, but that's another conversation entirely.)

Over time, I've learned to bear in mind that what appeals to my sense of the absurd might not play so well to everyone else. In an earlier draft of the story, Sheldon's confidence actually *decreased* over time. He started off with righteous anger, but by the time he went to the podium for that last speech, he was so apprehensive and exhausted that he decided to take a dive, replacing his original script with improvised nonsense. I loved the idea of building toward a big climax that completely pancaked. Later, after some test readers gave that idea a less-than-enthusiastic response, I decided to go for what I hope is a more satisfying conclusion. The muddled version of Kelly's speech that Shel tries to talk himself into giving is all that's left of that earlier version.

Another idea that went by the wayside was an interview, not unlike this one, with the adult Shel, so that readers could learn where he went after the close of the story. I wrote it but then chose not to include it, as I wanted to keep the focus on Shel's teenaged self.

What do you do with your time when you're not writing?

I was going to say something sensational like bare-knuckle boxing, but the truth is much less dramatic. When I'm not writing or being a librarian, I'm doing the usual domestic things, like hanging out with family and friends, riding my bike, doing chores (boo), reading, watching movies, cooking, and, of course, drinking coffee, around which my daily schedule revolves.

I collect records whenever time, space, and budget allow. It's part nostalgia, part thrill of the hunt, and part audiophilia—to me, vinyl just sounds better. Plus, every twenty minutes or so, you have to get up and flip the disc over, which counts as exercise.

Speaking of music, I don't exactly shred on the guitar but I get by. I keep one by my writing desk to be used for productive procrastination purposes. I love playing live, even though I tend to get paralyzing anxiety before I go on. For me, the best part of any show is when it's over—that's when I can say it was fun.

What else? I'm learning to bonsai, which I hope will help

me to be more patient. I also enjoy doing cryptic crossword puzzles—I think they do good things for your brain.

If readers were to compare your first book, M in the Abstract**, with this one, what sorts of things would you hope they'd notice?**

Their plots may be dissimilar but, thematically, I think there's a lot of crossover. In both books, the main characters are desperately holding on to the double-edged sword of their own secrets, refusing offers of assistance. Mary (from *M in the Abstract*) has these secret shadows that both comfort and torment her. Shel has his self-delusion, which allows him to live a life that is both comfortable and counterfeit. Facing their personal truths forces both characters toward a sense of self that is more authentic and not built around the worst kinds of lies, which are those that we tell ourselves.

Both books make use of internal dialogue. I like that technique, as it drops the reader right into the characters' heads, exposing their dilemmas and giving us a glimpse of how they view themselves. Mary is so conflicted and unstable that her inner dialogue usually takes the form of an argument. Shel is more of a problem solver—he tends to use his conversations with himself to try and improve his situation.

A handful of supporting characters from the first book

either make an appearance or are referenced in the second. There's really no need for them to be there, I just like the idea of the stories existing in the same universe. Some of these guest spots make sense, but one of them is a bit of a stretch. Never let it be said that I let a little thing like logic get in the way of some weird idea I have.

Are you willing to say what you're working on now?

Sure. I'm working on another teen novel called *Undertaking*, which is a sort of spiritual sibling to *M in the Abstract* and *Switch*. It's about Malcolm, a guy whose tragic history has closed him off emotionally. When his cranky guardian dies, Malcolm tries to conduct the funeral himself. Do you know what's involved in caring for a dead body? Do you want to know? Because it's really quite gross. Also, as I seem compelled to do such things, the story is constructed in alternating timelines, each moving at a different rate.

I've also been taking another crack at an experimental piece I wrote ages ago called *Vinegar16*, which consists of multiple copies of a letter on which most of the words have been blacked out. As you proceed, each page reveals a word or two or more, and the narrative and characters slowly develop over time. I quite like it, but it's very strange. I don't think anyone in their right mind would publish it.

I've been working on some comic book scripts, which, as a geek, is a lifelong dream of mine. They're still in the early stages so stay tuned, true believers.

How do you think being a parent and/or a librarian influences your writing?

I think it's made me more empathetic. When I was a teenager, and even into my twenties, my writing was bizarre and apocalyptic, drawing heavily (if not lifted wholesale) from the horror fiction, cult films, and post-punk music I favored at the time. I still like all of those things, and they obviously gave me something that I needed, but now I really want to be able to support young people in some small way, which is why I do what I do.

I'm around teens almost every day and I see their funny and sad and poignant moments. I see them moving in packs like perpetual-motion machines or sitting alone in their dark and private worlds. I see them holding hands as they leave the parking lot, only to have a break-up screaming match by the time they reach the sidewalk. It's such an intense time of life; every little bit of it seems important.

As a librarian, I see what's available to teens and I see what's not. There seems to be very little fiction that is specifically written around bisexuality. When I was doing my library studies, I did quite a lot of work in the area of LGBTQ fiction for teens, and it's cool to be adding my own novel to the genre

I've always enjoyed writing, but it wasn't until I was a parent that I started getting serious about it. What's the connection? I'm not sure. Maybe it's because being a parent puts you on a schedule, which I need. Or maybe I felt compelled to make more sense of our often senseless world for someone else's sake.